Volume Five

AIRSHIP 27 PRODUCTIONS

Sinbad-The New Voyages Volume Five

Published by Airship 27 Productions
www.airship27.com
www.airship27hangar.com

Interior illustrations © 2016 M.D. Jackson
Cover illustration © 2016 Terry Pavlet

Editor: Ron Fortier
Associate Editor: Steve Bennett
Promotions Manager: Michael Vance
Production and design by Rob Davis.

ISBN-13: 978-0692707579 (Airship 27)
ISBN-10: 0692707573

Printed in the United States of America

10 9 8 7 6 5 4 3 2 1

Sinbad
the New Voyages Volume 5

TABLE of CONTENTS

THE ISLAND OF THE PUPPET MASTER...5
By Barbara Doran
At the bidding of an old adversary, Sinbad and the crew of the Blue Nymph return an old wizard back to his home to battle a powerful efrit.

THE DESERT CONTEST...45
By Ron Fortier
With Sinbad off on his own adventure, Henri, Ralf and Tishimi are bound to get into some mischief of their own and that's exactly happens when two of them are kidnapped to fight in a gladiator like combat contest.

SINBAD & THE SINISTER STATUE......................................87
By Lee Houston Jr
Sinbad and his crew fall prey to countless traps as they attempt to salvage a long lost treasure.

SINBAD & THE DEVIL'S SEA..133
By Percival Constantine
Tishimi Osara becomes the crew's guide in an adventure that takes them to a long lost Japanese island where they confront a deadly shape shifting shaman queen.

ISLAND
of the
PUPPET MASTER
by Barbara Doran

The Inn of the Seven Stars was hidden away in the twisted streets of Bashir, at the furthest end of the darkest corner of that ancient port. So remote was it that those who never entered its weathered stone walls wondered how it survived. After all, an inn needed guests. How could such a place exist so far from the docks? It looked a hovel, its sign-board cracked in half, shutters askew.

Then there was its proprietor; dear Allah, its proprietor. Old as sin and twice as ugly, she was rarely seen, but that was more than enough. Bent over, twisted body concealed by her robes, most of her face was hidden by a veil. Only her eyes, deep set, and black as pitch could be seen. That, and wispy white locks that might once have been red. There was a smell about her, almost animal, and her hands were big, dark, and leathery, weathered by time and the sun.

Despite the inn's remote location and its strange owner, it had existed for as long as its neighbors could remember. And people did come; sorcerers, soldiers, spies. Big men, little men, the occasional woman. Guests who, down near the docks, would be carousing and fighting and wreaking havoc on the scenery. Guests who, ordinarily, always looked for trouble and found it.

One would think, with clientele such as these, the Inn of the Seven Stars would regularly require rebuilding. If it weren't shattered in a grand melee or set afire by some sorcerer's magic, it ought at least to attract the attention of the city guard. Yet none of these things ever came to pass, and those few in the neighborhood brave enough to visit refused to explain why this was so. They simply turned white and shuddered when asked.

Sinbad, Captain of the *Blue Nymph* and - depending on who you asked - a man of incredible courage or utter, callous, disregard for safety, eyed the Inn of the Seven Stars with interest. Beside him, Henri and Tishimi Osara looked upon it with near identical expressions of distrust. "I do not like this place," Henri said grimly. Short and lean, the brown-haired Gaul had a lazy look that hid the attention his archer's eye gave all it spied. Already he'd noted the location of every small child, every man and every woman - especially every woman - in the area. He'd also noticed seven cats sitting atop the roof of the inn, but cats were, after all, everywhere.

"If I understand correctly, though, it's the one place where our weapons are not only not needed, but not welcome." Sinbad grinned as he answered, teeth flashing bright in his dark-skinned face. "A place where enemies can meet safely, without fearing treachery." He stood before the door of the place with his characteristic élan, arms akimbo as he examined it thoughtfully. His shirt and loose pants were those of a commoner, but any who saw him would know him for far more. His scimitar alone was worth a fortune.

Tishimi touched the hilt of her katana. "I wonder, then, why you chose to bring myself and Henri for this... meeting." Her austere features had a disapproving expression. "Neither of us will willingly forgo our weapons." She was a small woman, dark haired, dark-eyed, dark clothed and dark humored. Though she went bare-faced in public, there wasn't a man who saw her would think she was readily available. Except, perhaps, the ever-optimistic Henri.

"Omar doesn't like the place, Haroun is too young and can you imagine what havoc Ralf would cause if he lost his temper?"

That brought a reluctant laugh to Henri's lips. "Well, yes, there is that. But the point remains, I am of a certainty not giving up my bow. And I would enjoy, from a distance, watching the result should anyone attempt to take our lovely Tishimi's blades. It would not be she who would be disarmed, I think."

Noting they were drawing attention from the neighbors, Sinbad shrugged off the question. "The only way to find out is to enter. And since we have been invited and since I have agreed to this meeting, I see no reason to come so far, only to falter at the doorway."

Past the rickety wooden door lay a small antechamber. Lit by a few guttering candles, two men were seated against the wall, appearing bored. The one was a muscular northerner in dark brown. He dwarfed his dark-haired little companion by several feet. Not that the little one was a weakling, being whipcord strong. Dressed in gray, his dark eyes and dark features had a sharp and dangerous look. Both men looked up incuriously, then returned to a game with strange skull shaped dice. Though burning with curiosity, Sinbad guessed these two were either the inn's guards or fellow guests awaiting their turn.

Looking around, Sinbad spotted a pair of great doors across the way. Covered in bright silver, they were elaborately decorated with a design of stars and triangles, the attractive pattern drawing the eye and almost seeming to have meaning behind it.

Before Sinbad could call for attention, a voice spoke from the shadows. "You are expected, Sinbad, you and your two companions."

Peering through the dark, all Sinbad could see was a faint shape, black against black. The voice was female, an old woman's, he thought, and he bowed in its direction. "Old mother," he said politely, "It seems there are those ahead of us." He indicated the two near the wall.

The smaller man spoke, his accent unfamiliar, "We wait for another," he said, "You aren't he. Go ahead. No point wasting gold on someone who might not come."

"Likely he's died again and we'll have to wait for his next incarnation, anyway," the big one added and Sinbad chose not to remark on the implications. This was a place, he sensed, where all sorts of strange beings might meet. Best not let one's curiosity be too obvious.

The old woman spoke again, "Your manners do your upbringing credit, Sinbad, but your party awaits you. Come."

Before Sinbad could follow the old woman, Tishimi raised a hand, dark eyes narrow. "I was told that no weapons were allowed in this place. I will not give up my blades, to you, or anyone."

A soft chuckle came from beneath the dark hood. "Child, I see no weapons."

Sinbad looked at Tishimi, startled, and realized that where her blades once rested was empty space. Another glance showed no sign of Henri's bow and angrily he reached for the hilt of his scimitar, seeing his companions do the same. To his relief, he found it where it should be and he opened his mouth to say as much. Except the old woman continued, "Within these walls, your weapons exist only to yourselves. Carry them as you will, they are useless as long as the spell that guards this place protects it. This is true for all who enter here. True, too, for any sorcerer who would use their magic against another."

Thoughtfully, Henri asked, "And if the spell is broken, what then?"

"All bets are off, boy. I can only do so much." The old woman chuckled. "Of course, it's remained strong for as long as I've been alive and that, my boy, is a long time indeed. Now, are you coming, or shall I tell your party you've changed your mind?"

Looking at the others only briefly before speaking, Sinbad said, "Lead on, old mother. My curiosity burns and I would know why one who has no love for me would have words."

The old woman guided them through a narrow hall that twisted and turned in ways that seemed impossibly tight. They passed door after door, all chased with silver and engraved with that strange pattern of stars and triangles, until Sinbad was sure they'd crossed their own path several times over. Yet, despite this, all they ever saw were walls and doors alongside them, never another corridor.

"Old mother, are we likely to be long?"

"The inn has been quite busy, lately. So many comings and goings," the robed and hooded figure said. "And there is only so much one person can do."

At last, the old woman stopped at one of the many doors, touching it with a diamond ring that glittered strangely against her thick, leathery, fingers. The door opened and Sinbad saw an attractive private room, a pot of tea steaming gently atop a mahogany table. The room's walls were covered the same design as the doors, all glittering in the light from several dozen candles. Jasmine scented the air, along with a faint metallic odor.

A figure stood on the other side of the table, a man of middling height, robed in heavily brocaded gold silk, his face was hidden beneath a helmet and mask that appeared to be made of brass. The mask was heavy, a face carved into the metal with a curly beard. It was a face Sinbad knew though he doubted the one behind the mask was he.

"Captain Sinbad el Ari," the man said, voice strangely metallic, "I greet and thank you for accepting the invitation." His speech was strangely stilted as if he had to think of each word before speaking it.

Sinbad eyed the man. "You are not my host," he said, remaining at the door.

"So it would appear. But my master is a man with enemies and he cannot leave his ship at this time. Thus, I have come in his place." The man bowed, "Allow me to introduce myself. I am Rasim, humble servant to Anwar abd Anwar, the Clockwork Sorcerer."

Once the old woman left them, Henri and Tishimi took up positions behind Sinbad. It was impossible to read Rasim's expression, but Sinbad thought their protectiveness amused their host. "Tell me," Sinbad said, pouring himself some tea and, after Rasim refused a cup for himself, sniffing it, "How am I to know you haven't poisoned the tea if you won't drink it?"

"I can't be poisoned, Sinbad. If you've not yet guessed, I am no more human than any of Anwar's other toys." Rasim lifted a hand to open his robe, revealing a torso formed of metal within which small gears turned. A soft whir could be heard now, quickly muffled when Rasim closed his robe once more. "Drink or not, Captain. It makes no difference to me."

Being nothing if not brave, or perhaps, as Tishimi claimed, foolhardy, Sinbad sipped the tea. "It is good," he said approvingly. "A tea worthy of the Emperor of China, I think." Indeed, unless his tongue betrayed him, this was the famous Imperial tea, a pound of which was worth a prince's ransom. "Very well, Rasim. Since your master is either unable or unwilling, to meet me, tell me what it is he wishes."

"You and Anwar have often been at odds."

That caused Henri to bark with laughter. "Odds? A mild way to put their dealings. Whenever they cross paths, your master comes out the worst."

"Mere details," Rasim countered.

"The bag of winds, and the race he lost because of it?"

"A minor setback."

"The eye of Sarsi?"

"A trifle."

"Princess Khasheera?"

Sinbad interrupted. "That was her Vizier's doing, not mine." Before the two could waste more time, he continued, "All of which was interesting but doesn't explain why Anwar wishes my assistance."

Rasim returned his attention to Sinbad. "Indeed. Then I continue. Anwar, loathe though he is to admit to any greater than he, cannot deny that even the largest of trees must begin as a small seed. When he was but a young man, he knew a sorcerer named Zahir al Sa'id. That sorcerer set his feet upon the path he now walks, and my master swore to repay him."

That could mean so many things and with a man like the Clockwork Sorcerer, Sinbad couldn't help but be suspicious. "Repay how?" And who was this Zahir, anyway? A sorcerer Anwar owed a debt to, no matter what sort, could hardly be a weakling himself. Yet Sinbad had never heard the name before.

"Zahir was cast out from a hidden land, many years ago. Away from it, he lost much of his mental capacity." There was an odd note in Rasim's voice, almost of regret. "His guidance and kindness were beyond price to Anwar. Without it, he would still be carving dolls for foolish and spoiled children. He swore, when he left Zahir, to help him return to his proper place, wherever it might be."

"I see. And he wishes me to find this place for him?" It made sense, there was nowhere upon the sea that Sinbad feared to sail.

"No. Anwar has secured the path already. Indeed, that is why he is unable to join you here. The one who cast Zahir from his home seeks to prevent his return. Anwar has sent for you, the most daring and most courageous of his rivals, to take Zahir back home." Rasim was twitching strangely and Sinbad realized a thin trail of smoke rose from his left nostril. "He... he... he... offers.... a bag of winds and a bottle of fire.... if you... will act... in his stead."

"What's happening?" Sinbad demanded, reaching instinctively for the weapon he knew he couldn't use. Behind him, Tishimi and Henri were doing the same.

"Anwar... is... under attack. The connection... is... breaking.... I must... have... your answer."

Sinbad hesitated only a moment. This was adventure and possibly a grand one. It was also an opportunity to have Anwar owe him a debt and that was not to be looked down on. And, of course, there was the payment itself. "For the things he offers, I will do what I can."

"T..t..take this device... go to... Aakkaaabaa Sss treee T. Find.... Zzzzhh zhh zhir...." Rasim was winding down, his entire body drooping where he sat. He set his empty hand upon the table and small metal being crawled out from his capacious sleeve and stepped forward. It stood but a hand and a half tall, its slim form that of a foreign god; one of the ones with a few too many hands and too many eyes. Silently it danced its way to Sinbad and held up its arms as if asking to be held.

When Sinbad hesitated, Rasim spoke again, twitching violently. "Taaake....It...willl...show...the way. It...knows...the path. Knows Zahir... was...his...once."

As Rasim fell from his seat, smoke rising from beneath his mask, Sinbad picked up the small statue. It cocked its head at him, gazing up with wide and strangely intelligent eyes. Only the third eye remained closed, squeezed tight shut as if it did not wish to see. It was warm in Sinbad's hand, the metal smooth and pleasant to touch.

"It feels alive," Sinbad said quietly to his companions as the statue crawled up to perch on his shoulder like a pet monkey. "And like trouble. Let's go, you two, I have a feeling we've no time to waste."

Bashir was a large city and Akaba Street was as far from the Inn of the Seven Stars as it could be without actually being in the bay. It was also a strange place to find a powerful sorcerer, being part of the Unveiled District. Here one could find all sorts of entertainments; wine - forbidden to any true follower of Allah; women - or boys, if so desired; and song - sometimes on key but most often not.

Entering the district, Sinbad noted the locals watching Tishimi with a certain wary caution that said they already knew better than to attempt anything with her. That was right, he'd sent her to retrieve Henri the last time they were there. Hopefully, the survivors had learned a valuable lesson about annoying Japanese swordswomen and learned it well. They had work to do and no time for dubious entertainment.

Which, of course, meant that Henri was flirting with each young woman they passed. Sinbad grabbed him by the elbow and marched him on. "Not now."

"But, Sinbad…."

"There isn't time."

Tishimi caught hold of Henri's other elbow and they made their way to Akaba Street. Once there, Sinbad was about to ask someone where he might find Zahir al Sa'id, but before he could, the statue sitting on his shoulder tugged his earlobe lightly. He glared at it, but all it did was point towards the middle of the street, where a makeshift stage had been set up. "He is there," it whispered softly.

The only figure on the stage was a big man with broad shoulders and a dark brown beard like a waterfall. As Sinbad stared, sure that could not be Zahir, the man shouted, "I present, with great joy, the beautiful, the marvelous, Malaika!" He stepped to the side, revealing a figure behind him, small, slight and hidden entirely by scarlet veils. Only pale, delicate, fingers were visible, each graced with rings of silver and gold.

Music played, coming from a trio of musicians seated along the back of the stage. For a moment it appeared as if the stage were much larger, giving the figure atop it more space. Then Sinbad realized the trio; a piper, a drummer and an oud player were small. Too small. Mere figurines about a third of a man's height, they were obviously clockwork.

The dancer began to move and now Sinbad and Tishimi had to hold Henri back. He was gazing up at the veiled figure with fascination. Nor could Sinbad blame him. The dancer's motions were as graceful and light as a gazelle's and as swift as a phoenix in flight. He could just see the shape of the dancer's limbs; slim, delicate and fragile, but nothing more. Malaika's veils, huge, fine banners of sheerest red and gold silk, fluttered too fast and hid too much.

The stage was surrounded by men and - to Sinbad's surprise - a few women. All watched the figure atop it hungrily, as if they each yearned to possess it. Yet - and this was a thing of wonder - not a one reached up to grasp at those veils. Not a one called out to claim the dancer's attention. Not a one climbed up on stage to join her.

The dance might have continued for some time, but a sound somewhere above them drew Sinbad's attention skyward. Something bright was approaching fast. No, not something, some things. There were dozens, screaming as they came. "HARPIES!"

As Sinbad rolled to the side, he knew he hardly needed to shout an order to his companions. Already Tishimi had her katana drawn, the blade glittering in the late afternoon sunlight. Already Henri had loosed his arrows, three in rapid succession. Already death had taken those monsters fast and foolhardy enough to attack first.

Seeing one of the harpies fall near him, an arrow buried neatly in the middle of her surprisingly beautiful forehead, Sinbad was surprised to see no blood. When a head, neatly removed from its shoulders by Tishimi's blade, rolled past, he realized why. The thing was not flesh, but a strange, glassy, substance like obsidian, oozing black liquid as it went.

A quavering voice shouted in a language Sinbad didn't recognize. Looking towards the stage, he saw an old man standing at its center, his arms spread wide as he spoke. At the same time the crowd scattered, disappearing into whatever nook or cranny or hidey-hole they could find. A sound like a wind rushing round them filled Sinbad's ears, though the air was still and calm. Then, as the old man collapsed into a heap, everything around them went mad.

Akaba Street was lined with impermanent structures; tents and small wagons. Canopies shaded goods lain out for potential buyers and banners proclaimed the presence of food, of household goods and other, less savory things. The poles and banners shifted in the still air, coming together until they tangled and twisted themselves into the shape of a man three times the size of Sinbad's friend Ralf Gunnarson. It raised itself above the crowd, towering protectively as it knocked harpies from the air.

Tishimi didn't hesitate. Recognizing an ally, she clambered up the thing's body to put herself in a better position to fight. It responded quickly, assisting her climb by lowering one arm and lifting her to its shoulder. Henri, having a longer reach with his bow, moved to hide behind one of its legs, using its bulk as a shield as he fired off shot after shot.

Noticing the harpies were aiming for the stage and two atop it, Sinbad dodged and rolled, cutting and stabbing as he went, until he'd joined them. The old man lay sprawled, his long white beard askew, with the dancer beside him, a tiny terrified figure hidden amidst her robes, her rings flashing as she cowered from their attackers. The three musician puppets were trying valiantly to protect the two, but their weapons were their instruments and already one had been torn to pieces.

"Fear not, fair maiden," Sinbad said. "I shall not allow any to harm you."

The girl said nothing, but her eyes, strange dark amber eyes, were wide as they watched him cut another harpy down. Then she crouched down, to let Sinbad stand above her and the sorcerer, his scimitar swinging in swift cuts designed to protect what lay beneath. His blade sang as it cut the air, slicing throats, wings and outstretched claws.

The giant caught hold of a harpy and held it for Tishimi to slay, a thing she did unhesitantly. Arrows took other harpies in the middle of their foreheads and knocked them from the sky. Until at last, bloodied and bruised, the defenders were victorious.

Gently, the giant set Tishimi down beside Sinbad. She bowed and for a moment it seemed it bowed in return. Then its myriad parts slid away like so many serpents, returning to their proper places. Within minutes, the empty street looked as if there'd been no fight. Except, of course, for the shattered bodies of the harpies. Then, as suddenly as they'd arrived, they melted away into puddles of black liquid that seeped into the ground and disappeared.

Sinbad turned his attention on the two he'd protected. The old man was stirring weakly and the girl lifted her head to look upon him with an unnervingly calm gaze. "Fair one," he said. "I must ask, is this the sorcerer Zahir al Sa'id?"

"He is called that by some," the girl agreed and Sinbad was struck by the slight, reedy, quality to her voice. It was not deep, but neither did it have the sweet, high, tones he'd have expected from one so delicate. "And

"I shall not allow any to harm you."

you, companioned as you are, can only be one man. I greet and thank you, Captain Sinbad, for your timely intervention."

The old man's eyes opened. Once green, they were blurred by cataracts and he put his hand out blindly, squinting as he tried to sit up. "Captain Sinbad?" he quavered. "What an odd thing. I dreamed you'd come."

"I am here on behalf of an old student of yours, sorcerer. He has asked me to find you and bring you home."

"Student? I had a student?" The old man sat up and now Sinbad could see how his hands shook and his head nodded uncontrollably.

"If you did, it was a very long time ago," the girl said. "Perhaps you do not remember."

"Yes. Yes. My memory fails me. What did he ask you to do again?"

Patiently, Sinbad told him, "He asked me to bring you home."

Zahir's bewildered expression was almost childishly confused. "Home? I have a home?" He made no motion to stand, staring at Sinbad with wide, near empty, eyes.

"Another thing from long ago, master," the girl said. "Would you like to go there?"

Though obviously lost, the old man sighed. "I... think... I should. You will take me?"

"Yes," Sinbad promised. "Yes, I will."

As Sinbad and Tishimi assisted the old man in standing, the big showman from earlier, the one who'd announced Malaika's performance, rushed up the stage. He put himself between Sinbad and the girl as if expecting him to carry her off. "What are you doing?"

"Taking this man home," Sinbad answered, a little surprised at the fellow's vehemence.

"Yes. Yes, going home, Ikal. Malaika should come."

"Malaika is my slave," the big man snapped and Sinbad saw the girl stiffen ever so slightly. "I have the papers to prove it. You sold her to me, remember?" He put an arm around Malaika possessively, a gesture the girl obviously resented. She looked sideways at her owner - if owner he truly were - and Sinbad thought her eyes flared with red-hot fury.

From Tishimi's expression she was about to step in and the result would not be pretty. Though tempted to let her gut the fat pig, Sinbad asked, "How much do you ask for her?"

Gold coins glittered in Ikal's eyes and he was about to suggest a price when Malaika spoke. "Do not waste your money on me, Sinbad. This greedy hog would ask far more than ever he gave Zahir."

"Malai...."

Malaika reached up and put a finger to Zahir's lips. "Hush. All will be well. Go with the nice sailor and let him take you where you need to go. You and I will be together again, soon enough. I promise you." Her voice was gentle, yet firm as a mother to her child. "Go quickly, Sinbad. His enemies hunt him still and now they will hunt him even more desperately."

Although both Tishimi and Henri looked as if they'd gladly argue the point further, Sinbad bowed to the girl. "As you ask, Rose of the Dawn. I will keep him safe for you."

"Do that, and it will not be just Anwar abd Anwar who owes you a debt," Malaika said. Only later did it occur to Sinbad that he had never mentioned the sorcerer's name.

The *Blue Nymph's* last adventure, profitable though it'd been, had done some damage to both the ship and the crew. New seamen must be hired, sails and ropes must be repaired or replaced, and food and water acquired. All took time and Sinbad hoped Zahir's enemy, whoever they were, was slowed by the loss of their harpies.

"Your master's bag of winds would be useful," he told the statue sitting on his desk. All four of its hands twitched in a shrug that said it had no answer. "Rasim said you know the way to this island? And what is the name of the place, anyway?"

"Dumiya, the Island of Twilight, lost in the Sea of Night all these many years," the statue said, voice thin and flute-like.

Omar, Sinbad's First Mate and oldest friend stiffened. "Sinbad, even if we can navigate the Sea of Night, which has neither moon nor stars to guide us by, the Island of Twilight is ruled by the Puppet Master! Do you have to walk us straight into legend at every turn?"

Sinbad grinned. No doubt the difficulty navigating the Sea of Night was why Anwar chose not to risk his flying ship, nor his own flesh, to this venture. "We've faced many such dangers," he reminded Omar. He didn't mind his friend's caution. If anything, the short, pugnacious, sailor's conservative ways acted as counterpoint to his own more reckless ones. "But who is this Puppet Master you speak of?"

With a fierce frown as he tried to remember the details, Omar told him, "The stories say he is a terrible efrit, banished from his own kind for crimes unknown. Exiled and alone, he has built hundreds, perhaps thousands, of magical puppets to companion him and protect him from intruders."

"Puppets?" Sinbad repeated thoughtfully. "Clockworks?"

"How the devil am I to know?" Omar shook his head. "The point is, if Zahir comes from that island, he might be the Puppet Master himself!"

Mad and confused as Zahir al Sa'id was, Sinbad doubted it. Admittedly, his sorcery was similar to this Puppet Master's powers. Yet he was obviously just a bewildered old man, no efrit, nor even jinn. "Statue... what do I call you?" he asked.

"Murshid will do well enough," the statue said. "It would be rude, and dangerous, to call me by the name of the God whose form I wear."

Agreeing wholeheartedly, Sinbad pointed to the map upon his wall. Drawn on dozens of fine pieces of parchment, carefully mounted and framed, it showed the world as he knew it; with all the places he'd traveled. "Guide. An auspicious name for your purpose, Murshid. Show me the way we must travel to reach the Sea of Night. And tell me all you know about it, and the Island of Twilight."

"The Sea of Night," Murshid said as Sinbad carried him over to the map, "is a world beyond our world. As your First Mate has said, it is a place without light except that which you carry with you. There is no land within it, only endless water."

It was Omar who protested, "No land? But what of the Island of Twilight?"

"The Island of Twilight is formed of flotsam and jetsam. It drifts, aimlessly, upon the Sea of Night, having been taken there by the one who rules it now." Before Omar could open his mouth to protest again, Murshid spread his four arms in a calming gesture. "I have a way to find it, sir. Once we enter the Sea of Night, I will open my eye and seek. It will be risky; the island's ruler may notice and send his minions against us once more. And on the Sea of Night, he is far more powerful than he is here."

Omar muttered under his breath, then said more loudly, "And how, in Allah's name, are we to know you tell the truth? What if this whole mess is the Clockwork Sorcerer's trap, set to put us where we can no longer be a thorn in his side?"

"You do not know," Murshid admitted. "Nor can I offer any proof but my word. And that, given I am only a sorcerer's tool, is not much use, I fear. But this I will say. Zahir's enemy now knows Sinbad has involved himself in his affairs. The good Captain's reputation precedes him. Even if you could convince him to leave this task to my master, the enemy knows that he does not run from danger. He will be certain Sinbad is on his way and seek destruction—of Sinbad, his crew and his ship as well."

"Which means," Sinbad said grinning, the excitement, and danger of the adventure setting his pulse racing, "That we may as well go. Trust me, Omar. Have I ever steered you wrong?" The look on Omar's face answered that question only too well.

It took very little time to set the *Blue Nymph* in order. Within hours of Sinbad's return, she was sailing out of the bay and out along the coast. The Sea of Night, according to Murshid, could only be reached by entering the rock formation called the Seven Sisters and, at the exact moment of noon, leave it again through the correct path. Murshid, again, would be their guide in this.

In the meantime, Omar spent his time making sure the new crew was properly settled and assigned. He'd had quite a time choosing them. Those who traveled with Sinbad knew their fortunes were made should they survive the trip. Some, however, thought to make their fortunes quickly, without risk, by means less fair than simple survival.

Omar had learned to recognize undesirable crewmen, as well as the starry-eyed would-be adventurers with strong arms and near total ignorance of what it was to crew a vessel such as the *Blue Nymph*. He'd turned away easily half of those who'd come aboard seeking employment. Those remaining he set working hard and long, on the theory that tired men made less trouble.

The next morning was bright and clear, as beautiful a day as one might ask for. Sinbad stood at the wheel, watching the waters, listening to the constant murmur of the sea, the sound of the wind in the sails and inevitably, an argument between two of his most trusted companions drifting up from somewhere below deck.

This time it was Henri and Haroun, two men who - generally - got along well enough. Haroun was a quiet youth whose long eye and quick wits made him invaluable as a lookout. He didn't womanize like Henri, nor drink at all, so there were seldom times when they disagreed. That, alone, was more than enough reason to investigate.

Handing the wheel off to Omar, Sinbad snuck down the steps below deck, moving slow and quiet so as not to attract the two men's attention. Thus, he was able to hear Haroun say, "You have to tell the Captain."

"I've done nothing that is wrong, boy. Leave it be."

"Henri, you know you can't do things like this. Bringing a woman aboard...."

"A woman, Henri? At a time like this?" Sinbad broke into the conversation, walking forward to stand over the two smaller men. "What are you thinking? Are you thinking?"

The look of chagrin on Henri's face was one Sinbad was wearily resigned to. "It is not as it seems, Sinbad, I swear this to you!"

Haroun turned. "Sir! I promise I wouldn't help him keep it secret. But I thought he should be the one to tell you!" His young face, surrounded by a cloud of curly black locks, had the most earnest of expressions.

"Run along, Haroun," Sinbad told him firmly. "It's your turn for the watch, anyway, isn't it?" It wasn't, actually, but it was as good excuse as any to get the lad out of the way. Only when Haroun had hurried off did Henri have the grace to look terribly embarrassed as Sinbad asked, "Well?"

"It's that dancer. Malaika begged me to help. Said they wouldn't let her join the crew."

"Another girl.... wait... she tried to join the crew? A girl?"

"She would not be the first to try that trick," Henri pointed out and Sinbad admitted it was true. "She said she escaped that pig, Ikal and came here to be with her grandfather."

The relationship between the two hadn't been stated, but Sinbad wasn't surprised to learn it, as unhappy as Zahir seemed to have been to leave Malaika behind. He'd never protested, barely said a word since he'd boarded, but it was obvious he was lost without her. "I would have bought her," he pointed out. "Now we're going to have that fat fool after us for theft."

"We're far enough from port now, I doubt me he can do a thing," Henri shrugged. "And I would have told you she was aboard, once we were safely past the Seven Sisters."

"And you'd had time for some dalliance," Sinbad added knowingly. This wasn't the first time Henri had done such a thing, after all. The fact it infuriated the crew only made the idea more attractive to the Gaul. He lived for being in trouble. Which, of course, was probably why the two of them were friends. "Well, take me to her and let us learn how she managed to escape Ikal."

Henri led Sinbad through the ship. "She's beautiful, beneath those veils,

Sinbad. A fragile flower, as delicate as a Chinese ivory. I hardly dared to touch her." He might have gone on, touting Malaika's virtues, but for the fact that, when he gently pushed aside the canvas he'd used to cover her hideaway and looked in, all they found there was dust.

Concerned one of the rougher sailors might find Malaika and be less considerate than Henri; Sinbad immediately ordered the ship searched from top to bottom. To his deep surprise and chagrin, however, no sign could be found. It was as if she'd vanished into mist. Fearing now that one of the crew was either concealing her or, worse, had murdered her and thrown her overboard, Sinbad searched the ship himself, commanding all to remain at their posts.

Yet still there was no sign, though he searched the ship several times over. Malaika was a tiny thing, true, but there wasn't a nook, nor cranny, he didn't check. Tishimi questioned the crew, her dark eyes watching faces for lies or misdirection and finding nothing. No one, from the twin cooks to the big carpenter, knew where Malaika was or what had happened to her. Nor was there sign of struggle, veil, nor blood.

It was almost noon when Sinbad accepted he wasn't going to find Malaika. Either she'd gone overboard or she was beyond skilled at concealment. Being Zahir's granddaughter, it was possible she was a sorceress herself, with spells to hide behind. Whatever the truth, they were less than a day from the Seven Sisters and they had no time for fruitless search.

Gazing at the sea usually calmed Sinbad's spirit and he let the play of light on water draw his attention as they sailed. A strange thought occurred to him and he turned to Omar. "Why was our cook's twin here in Bashir to be hired?" They'd hired the first twin two ports earlier, after their last cook had married into the family of the local innkeeper. Sinbad was certain there'd only been one new man at that stop.

"Eh? By Allah's beard, what do you mean, Sinbad? The cook's an only child!"

Sinbad closed his eyes, remembering his discussion with the cook in the kitchen and the second cook down in stores. He'd asked why the man had left his post when he'd been ordered to remain in place and the second man had claimed to be the other's twin. A chill ran up his spine and he tightened his lips. Both were short men, identical in every way. The only difference between the two was their eyes, hazel for the one, reddish gold for the other.

"Damnit! That was Malaika! She's an illusionist!" Sinbad turned, intending to order all hands on deck, when Haroun suddenly shouted, "Sea serpent, dead ahead!"

Sea serpents were rare in these waters. Usually they followed whale pods, hunting the huge creatures like tigers hunted deer. Yet sometimes they found their way into the shallower waters near land, where they often mistook ships for their preferred prey.

The more experienced sailors caught hold of long poles, taking up positions around the ship. At the same time, Sinbad, guided by Haroun's calls, shifted their direction, hoping to avoid the monster before it arrived. This was nothing new and he felt little worry over the attack.

It was only when the sea serpent, a long bodied beast, green-blue and covered in seaweed lifted itself above them that Sinbad realized it was no ordinary monster. Usually sea serpents, being four times as long as Ralf, would arch themselves over the deck of the ship and down the other side, trying to wrap itself around as they would a whale.

This serpent, however, raised its head high above the rail and stared down upon the crew with angry red eyes. There was a mind behind those eyes, Sinbad would swear, and an evil one at that. Moreover, he'd seen that look before, in the eyes of the harpies that had hunted the sorcerer Zahir.

An arrow buried itself in one of the serpent's eyes, the second striking its tough and scaled hide as it jerked back rapidly. It screamed at Henri's attack, lifting itself higher and darting its head forward, jaws wide as it tried to catch the archer in its mouth.

Before the serpent could reach Henri, the Gaul rolled backwards. "Only turn its head and I can get the other eye," he called.

Somehow the serpent seemed to sense that danger, for every time Henri moved, it twisted its head out of danger. At the same time Ralf, his axe cutting at the monster's neck, chipped slowly away at a giant scale. He was singing as he chopped, one of those strange, barbaric, songs of his people, and Sinbad was glad someone was enjoying themselves. The big Viking lived for moments like this.

The *Blue Nymph* bounced and shuddered as the serpent slithered up onto her. The crew were doing their best, pushing its coils off with their gaffs, but it just slipped away and back again. More and more of the serpent's body covered the deck, pushing the *Blue Nymph* down and nearly swamping her.

Angry, because the *Blue Nymph* was the most beloved of all his companions, Sinbad leapt for the serpent's torso, climbing it like a palm tree, his knees and hands clutching tight as he struggled for its head. If he could just get to its other eye he could end this fight, or so he hoped.

The serpent shifted around to evade Ralf's axe, sliding up over the *Blue Nymph's* figurehead. Wood creaked and Sinbad winced for his beloved ship. Then he realized the creaking wasn't from the pressure of the serpent's body against the fragile wood. Instead, the mermaid's arms lifted to catch hold of the seaweed wrapped around the serpent's torso. Like so many small snakes the seaweed twisted upwards towards the serpent's head.

Realizing his chance, Sinbad grabbed hold and let the seaweed carry him along, until he was perched atop the monster's head with one clear shot at its remaining eye. He struck hard, fast and true, his blade burying itself deep into the eye and the brain beyond.

A moment later the serpent disappeared in a rain of black liquid and Sinbad found himself dropping straight for the sea. To the side would have been safe, for he could swim readily, but he was right ahead of the ship. She would have sailed right over him had he fallen in. Fortunately, strong hands caught him, lifting him up to see his rescuer.

The beautiful face of the *Blue Nymph's* figurehead smiled at him, a pert and impish grin that - in his mind - was exactly as it should be. Then her hands carried him to the side so he could grab the rail. Someone stood there; fragile, gem covered fingers touching the figurehead's shoulder. Small and slight, with eyes as red as the reddest amber, he, for he seemed a man, was dressed in black silks, with loose, silky black hair. He smiled, a smile that hid a universe of secrets, and disappeared in a trail of ruby tinted mist.

Sinbad's cabin was packed. Most of his companions were there, with the exception of Rafi and Byrne. The one patching up the crew, while William guarded Zahir al Sa'id. It was obvious someone sought the sorcerer's life. Having been thwarted twice, there was no telling what they'd do now.

Besides, there was a chance that Malaika might find her way to her grandfather's cabin. If so, Sinbad wanted the Celt's sharp eyes there to catch her, should she make an appearance. He had his suspicions about her nature and had no wish to let her wander his ship unhindered. Meanwhile, there were other things to consider and Sinbad turned his attention to the discussion.

"What sort of being is the enemy?" Tishimi asked Murshid, kneeling on the floor in front of Sinbad's desk. Henri was squeezed on one end of Sinbad's bunk, with Haroun at the other. Ralf, too tall to stand straight in that small space, was crouched in a corner while Omar stood in another and Sinbad sat behind his desk.

Murshid, the only one settled comfortably, lay atop a paperweight in a pose resembling an amused Rajah, waving one of his four hands amiably. "I don't exactly know because my master does not know. Zahir once spoke of how he was thrown from his land by that being, but even he wasn't sure who it was. Of course, Zahir never has been entirely clear, even in those days. Loss of his land appears to have fractured his mind."

Zahir did, indeed, appear to be nearly incapacitated. It left Sinbad wondering how he'd managed that spell, back on Akaba Street. For that matter, who had cast the spell that had aided Sinbad's fight with the sea serpent? If Zahir, he was powerful indeed, given he'd been sleeping in his cabin at the time.

Murshid continued, marking his point with tiny fingers. "My master believes the enemy is an efrit. What else would be powerful enough to drive a sorcerer like Zahir from his home and break his mind?"

"Sounds like an interesting fight," Ralf growled through his thick blond beard. "Bring it on. We've battled worse."

Sinbad smiled as the others rolled their eyes at Ralf's enthusiasm. "We won't know what, exactly, we face until we reach the island," he admitted. "Tishimi, do you have any thoughts on the matter?"

"There's one thing," she told him. "We have been attacked twice and never at night. Surely it'd be wiser to send minions when the odds are against us. Is it possible the enemy can only attack us when the way is opened?"

It made sense. Thinking more on the matter, it occurred to Sinbad that the second attack had been closer to noon than the first. He said so, adding, "If that's true, the moment the portal opens and we try to go through it, the enemy will be waiting for us."

"It is in my thoughts that the attacking force is larger each time," Henri said. "Which means whatever hunts us next will be worse than a sea serpent. Is there a way to sneak past, I wonder?"

Sinbad didn't get a chance to answer. The door opened and Byrnes came stalking in, drawing a slim figure behind him, his stubby fingers

"….master believes the enemy is an efrit."

wrapped around the fine-boned wrist of a girl dressed in sailor's breeches and a loose-fitting linen shirt. "Caught her. As you expected, trying to sneak into Zahir's room to hide beneath his bed."

Blue eyes stared pleadingly at Sinbad from a delicate face framed by soft and curly golden hair. Looking on her, Sinbad could see how she'd convinced Henri to bring her aboard. She was very much his type, a woman of the north, it seemed, pale-skinned, slightly built and as fine as porcelain. And yet there was a wrongness about her, though Sinbad could not place a finger why he thought so.

"Malaika?" he asked, cautiously. Perhaps it was not her after all?

Her voice confirmed the name. "Indeed," she said, in that odd, reedy, tenor that had attracted his attention before. Sinbad doubted anyone could have imitated it so readily. "I apologize, I truly do, but I could not let Zahir go alone. He needs me."

Since Sinbad had been fully prepared to pay for her freedom, he could hardly claim she was unwelcome. He could, and did, say, "You should have let me buy you."

"Ikal didn't own me." Glancing at Tishimi, Malaika added, "There would have been bloodshed, had I spoken. And that would have brought the city guard upon us. There wasn't time and I knew I could escape him on my own. Which, as you see, I did."

Smiling, amused at the girl's frankness, Sinbad told her, "Yes, you did. And now you're here, perhaps you can answer some vexing questions."

The girl inclined her head. "I can only try."

"First, do you know who it is that sends these monsters against us?"

"Zahir's enemy, the ruler of the Island of Twilight."

"The Puppet Master." They already knew that much. "But who is he... or she?"

Malaika raised a gilded eyebrow and seemed to bite back her response. Then, gently, she said, "I did not say my master's enemy is the Puppet Master." When Sinbad spread his hands, asking her to continue, she explained, "The one who rules the island now is a usurper who took advantage of the Puppet Master in a moment of weakness, breaking him and casting him from his place. And before you ask, no, Zahir al Sa'id is not the Puppet Master himself, though they are the same kind."

Since that would have been Sinbad's next question he fell silent. Fortunately, Tishimi had another, "This usurper, who is he?"

"An efrit, Lady Tishimi. One of the fallen followers of Iblis. He came to the island to steal its power and, as his sendings prove, succeeded."

"His name?"

"My lady, knowing an efrit's name is the same as mastering it. If I could put name to the usurper then weak and frail though I am, even I could defeat him."

Such was common knowledge and, indeed, had saved them at least twice in the past. "I have a question, beauteous one," Henri said and when Malaika eyed him coquettishly, added, "No, not that... at least not right now."

She chuckled, a soft ripple of sound. "Do go on, my dear sir."

"If your grandfather is not the Puppet Master and given his obvious infirmity, why is it that this usurping efrit seeks so desperately to slay him?"

"Because," Malaika said, her expression proud, "He came into this world to seek the efrit's name and, indeed, he found it. But his mind was injured in the process and he is unable to tell it to me, that I might stand against that evil beast. There is a device to heal him, on the Island of Twilight, where he was born."

"Then," Sinbad said quietly, "we must get him there quickly. One last question, Flower of Dawn. The enemy sends his minions against us through the very portal, we must pass to reach the island. Do you know a way to distract him?"

Thoughtfully, Malaika said, "What you ask is no simple thing, and right this moment I am not sure. But I promise you, oh master adventurer, before the portal opens next, when we prepare to pass through the Seven Sisters and into the Sea of Night, I will have your answer for you."

That night, Omar allowed the crew to sit up and - quietly - enjoy what might be their last sight of the stars and moon. He even, despite his better judgment, allowed Malaika to dance for the crew, Henri, and Tishimi providing the music on guitar and flute.

Only when the crew had been sent to their bunks and the others had gone to do whatever it was they did at night, did Sinbad find his way to the prow of his vessel, where Malaika stood silently gazing towards the distant shapes of the Seven Sisters, just visible on the horizon.

They were quiet several moments but Sinbad finally asked, "Tell me, Malaika, if that is your real name, are you a man or a woman?"

She eyed him with a sideways slant and her lips were curved in a sweet and secret smile. "What sort of question is that? Is the answer not obvious?" She indicated her lithe figure with a graceful gesture.

"You are an illusionist, perhaps even a shape-shifter, Malaika. Allah may know whether that admittedly lovely form is truly yours, but I do not."

"Is it companionship you seek?" She sounded deeply amused and more than a little interested. "I am well practiced in the arts of the bedchamber. I have had many years to perfect my skills."

Voice a little hard, for he would not lie to himself and pretend he didn't feel the force of her, Sinbad said, "It is this, Malaika. Right now your eyes are bluer than the bluest sky and your hair pure gold. You are, in every way, the very thing Henri seeks. Oh, he loves all women, but your face, your form, everything about you reminds him of the girls back home."

"And?"

"Your eyes were not blue when I first met you. They were purest of red amber. Indeed, they could even have been called ruby, for the briefest of moments."

"And?"

"And the man who stood here, casting a spell I am certain, beyond all certainty, brought life to my ship's figurehead and saved my life, had red eyes. Not to mention rings like the ones you wear now."

"So?" There was a world of amusement in the woman's voice and Sinbad turned to put a hand upon her shoulder. He did not grip tightly, though he was severely tempted to shake her. Especially when she smiled.

"I want to know what you are. Efrit? Jinn? Angel? Ghul? You are not what you seem and I am putting my crew's life in your hands."

Slowly the gold hair straightened and darkened, becoming the silky dark locks he'd seen before. The face changed only slightly, skin lightening until its resemblance to porcelain was impossible to ignore. Touch it, Sinbad suspected, and it would be like stroking the finest of bone-china. Her body changed as well, becoming a bit more slender, until she resembled nothing so much as a sexless doll dressed in black.

"None of the above. Nor can I tell you what I am, because, in truth, I do not know. My creator is long disappeared from all the worlds." Malaika's smile had a distant, almost lonely look to it. "As for your other questions, yes and yes, or no and no. Both and neither. Would you care to test it?"

Realizing that, even now, Malaika was quietly offering her, his, itself, Sinbad stepped back. "I was not seeking that from you."

"If rumor speaks true, you have slept with a Goddess, with priestesses. You have even kissed a ghul, though she wore a princess's shape at the time. Am I so terrible that you dare not look upon me? I promise I can be whatever you desire."

"Is this a distraction?"

"Of course. Tomorrow we go into the Sea of Night to face the efrit who shattered the master of the Island of Twilight and cast him from his throne. Tomorrow, if we fail, I will die. What else would it be, but a distraction?" Malaika chuckled softly at Sinbad's startled expression as she added, "You need not fear my becoming overly attached, Captain. I already know there is but one true love in your life."

She reached out and took his hand, her fingers strangely warm. "But fortunately, Captain, dear Captain, she shares."

By mid-morning the next day the *Blue Nymph* was in sight of the Seven Sisters. Once the crater of a now extinct volcano, the walls had been broken and eroded by the sea, leaving seven pillars in a rough circle around a strangely still, deeply blue, basin. Long ago an unknown race had carved those pillars, so that now, seven robed and hooded figures stood atop the weathered stone.

Standing at the *Blue Nymph's* prow with Tishimi and Murshid, the little statue seated elegantly on Tishimi's shoulder, Sinbad asked, "So we must be within that circle by noon and, when the portal opens, enter it? Is that really all there is to it?"

"Well," Murshid admitted, "it's a bit more complicated. Otherwise people would be falling through that hole all the time. But never fear, I can guide you."

Noticing something atop the outstretched hand of one of the Sisters, Sinbad peered upwards. He was about to shout for Haroun when the object moved, glittering in the sunlight as it flew down to the *Blue Nymph*. It only took a moment to recognize it as one of Anwar abd Anwar's clockwork gryphons, ridden by Rasim.

The automaton landed upon the deck of the *Blue Nymph* and immediately sent his mount flying off again. "Captain, permission to come aboard?"

"You seem to have done so already," Sinbad pointed out dryly. "I see you've recovered from your recent breakdown."

"I am repaired, yes. I've come to help you on this venture into the Sea of Night. As well as give you your reward." Rasim held out a small, ornate, box, opening it to reveal a velvet bag and a bottle whose contents seemed to flare and swirl like fire.

Sinbad eyed the items without taking them. "I've not yet finished my side of the bargain," he pointed out. "And I don't remember asking for help."

"To be honest, Anwar is curious. He wishes to know what power it is that can usurp the throne of the Puppet Master. As for the reward, you may need it, where you're going. Anwar trusts you will complete your side of the bargain because you are you."

With a sigh, Sinbad made a gesture towards the Seven Sisters. "Well then, perhaps you have an answer to our current dilemma. The enemy sends his monsters to attack us through the portal. How are we to get past without being torn apart when it opens next?"

That seemed to stump the automaton and he turned to look, cocking his head thoughtfully. "I am not sure."

"Malaika said she'd think on the subject," Tishimi pointed out. "Or is she still with Henri, insatiable creature that she is?" Zahir's granddaughter had been speaking with the Gaul earlier that morning and the two hadn't been seen since.

"I have made my peace with Henri already," Malaika said, appearing out of nowhere to perch elegantly beside the *Blue Nymph's* figurehead. She, and Sinbad decided to think of her so, despite appearances, wore the thin, dark, form that resembled nothing so much as an ivory statue garbed in black silk. At Tishimi's raised brow, Malaika indicated her doll-like body. "This is the truest of my forms, milady. I will need all my power for other things, and soon."

"That," Murshid muttered, "and a shape that doesn't make every male within sight forget their duty in favor of ogling her."

Malaika ignored the statue, turning her attention on Sinbad with a smile. "The only way I can think to distract any monster the enemy sends against us is to bait it elsewhere." Sinbad raised a brow, encouraging her to continue and she gestured below. "Have your men bring out any extra sails, extra wood, extra anything and I will create that bait. It will not be nearly as beautiful as your lovely vessel, but I promise you, it will give us the few minutes needed."

"Of course," Rasim exclaimed, drawing Malaika's intent gaze, "That portal isn't open for very long. Once we're through, and it closes, the enemy's monster will be trapped on the wrong side."

That wouldn't protect them from the enemy once they were in his territory but Sinbad could see the sense. "Omar!" he shouted. "Bring up anything we don't need! Cloth, wood, anyone who doesn't move fast enough! We have a plan!"

Just short of noon enough spare items had been found and thrown overboard. Holding a rope attached to the boards, Malaika exerted her sorcery upon the mess floating beside them, drawing the boards and ropes and cloth together into a shape both like and unlike the *Blue Nymph*. Its outline was true, so that seen from a distance it would look like Sinbad's ship to one who'd never seen it before. Close up, however, it was obviously a twisted, tangled, collection of junk, too small to be a proper ship.

"One last thing," Malaika said. "It must move of its own and I cannot be here for that." She held out her hands and tapped one wrist lightly with a suddenly sharpened fingernail, so that blood, or what appeared to be blood, beaded upon the pale surface of her skin. Then it fell to the deck of the smaller ship and spread, darkening to near black as it seeped into the wood.

The figurehead of the lure ship raised its head and looked at Malaika, its eyes glowing soft purple. It made a noise, a quiet, sad little sound. "Yes, child," Malaika said. "I know. Survive and come to me when you can." The wooden head bowed obediently and the little ship suddenly moved in the water, gliding away from the Seven Sisters.

"So you share your grandfather's gift, Malachi?" Rasim said suddenly, watching Malaika closely.

"So it would appear, servant of Anwar," Malaika answered. "Captain, we should be going. I shall use my illusions to conceal us from view until we've passed through the portal."

Agreeing, Sinbad took up the wheel, shouting orders to the crew as he guided the ship between the nearest two sisters. Inside the circle they formed, their faces were almost visible beneath the shadow of their hoods, yet somehow Sinbad had no desire to see them clearly.

As the sun moved higher Murshid perched upon the wheel, using every arm to keep himself upright. "Aim your ship for that Sister there." At Sinbad's sudden stare, the statue added, "You will not break upon the rocks, Captain. The portal opens through her."

Before Sinbad could answer, or complain that Murshid might have warned him, the air around that Sister shimmered and strange black light flared into a near perfect circle. Something moved within the darkness beyond, then a great head slid out of the shadows. More insect than fish, the creature glided out of the portal to circle around the center, staring downwards intently. It was long, with many legs, and seemed to have the power of flight, despite a notable lack of wings. It glittered, iridescent in the sunlight and Sinbad reflected that it was almost, almost, attractive. Except, of course, for the huge maw that opened and closed as it hunted for its prey.

At the forefront of the *Blue Nymph*, Malaika spread her hands, body glowing a soft red. Sinbad held his breath, for he had no desire to face a monster that size without better weapons. To his relief, Malaika's illusion fooled the creature. It swung around and raced out of the circle towards Malaika's false ship.

"Now," Murshid said. "Before the portal closes."

"Give me a wind, Tishimi!" Sinbad ordered and the warrior moved quickly, taking a knotted strand from the bag Rasim had given Sinbad and cutting it in pieces with several slices of her blade. Then, using the power the spell granted her, she stared intensely straight at the portal.

Immediately, the *Blue Nymph* leaped across the water, gliding fast and smooth, driven by Tishimi's wind straight into the portal and to the darkness on the other side. As the portal closed behind them, leaving them in a blackness deeper and colder than any Sinbad had ever experienced before, Rasim coughed as if to clear his throat. "You know," he said. "If you just untie the knot you can use them again."

The Sea of Night was as dark as predicted. Above and below seemed a void made all the more terrifying by the way the water failed to reflect so much as a glimmer. It was as if the *Blue Nymph* floated in a sphere of ink. Had the light of their torches and braziers failed to cut the blackness surrounding them, Sinbad knew he'd have a mutiny on his hands.

The cold posed another problem. Accustomed to the warmth of their sunlit lands, Sinbad's crew were shaking and chilled so that every blanket and cloth not used in making Malaika's false ship was now in use as extra covering. Malaika took it worse than the rest, her fragile body almost unable to move against the intense chill. Only Ralf, born in far colder climes, was unaffected and his cheerful mockery somehow gave everyone reason to keep moving, if only so they could find the energy to hit him for it.

Omar decided rowing was the best solution to keeping them warm. They complained, vociferously, but quickly found he was right. Between the exercise and the braziers set to heat the galley, the rowers were probably the most comfortable of all.

Still standing atop Sinbad's wheel, Murshid was finally doing what he'd come to do. His third eye, so long closed, would open briefly so he could look at something only he could see, then guide Sinbad's hand as he steered the ship. "Port. Further port. Straight again," he said. Several times it seemed to Sinbad as if they'd gone in circles, but in this dark, who could tell?

Unaffected by the cold, Rasim stood behind Sinbad and complained, "Really. Those strands are hard to make. And expensive. Phoenix down, dragon's breath, the root of a moly plant. Is that what you did the last time? Just cut them up for tinder?"

"The knots are too tight," Sinbad countered. "And we didn't have time to undo them. Now, or then."

Rasim shook his head, the firelight glittering off his metal mask with every movement. "Such a waste."

"Port again," Murshid said. "No, more than that."

"I swear we're going around in circles."

"We are," Murshid assured him. "If you could see what I see, you'd understand why."

"Try describing it," Sinbad suggested. If nothing else, it was better than listening to Rasim.

The statue considered his answer. "The sea appears to be flat here, but that's because we're sitting in the valley of a wave - of sorts. If you went off too far to the side, you'd be lifted up and capsized."

"I still don't understand."

"The sea vibrates to a song you cannot hear," Murshid sighed. "Without light, you're not going to see it and I don't have the tools to explain."

"All right. Then do you know why that water doesn't reflect anything?"

Murshid turned his head all the way so he could glare straight at Sinbad, his third eye glowing the same bright red as Malaika's. "Are you acquainted with the properties of light and matter? No? Then yes, I know and no, I can't explain that either."

"The sea vibrates to a song you cannot hear."

"Then another question. Any thoughts on why the enemy isn't attacking us yet?"

Malaika raised her head. She'd been dealing with the cold in her own way, by sitting - unharmed - in a brazier absorbing its heat. Already she'd gone through three lightings and by the look of her would happily take more. "The monster he sent against us was enormous, Sinbad. The power to create it from these waters and send it so far away, equally so."

"These waters? Can he transform this sea and turn it against us?"

"No." Malaika eyed the darkness around them, adding, "To transform the entire sea would take more power than even the Puppet Master at his strongest could have summoned. As it is, the enemy won't be able to create another monster until his power is restored."

Relieved, Sinbad asked, "So we have time?"

"We have until portal opens again. If we don't get Zahir safely restored and learn the enemy's name, not only will that other monster return, but the enemy will have the power to create another. I'd rather not find out what he sends against us next."

Sinbad might have answered, but after the long, intense, darkness, he was seeing a soft glow off to port. A black hill, hidden against the black sky, sloped down and at Murshid's guidance, they rounded it to find themselves approaching a sphere set in the middle of a forest of black spikes. It was surrounded by mounds and mounds of floating debris that Sinbad recognized as the broken parts of ships and cargo. Things moved on those mounds, twisted silhouettes that put Sinbad in mind of skeletons and dead things and a smell of sulfur filled the warming air.

As for the sphere itself, it glowed like a blood-red moon, the only other light in the darkness. "That," he asked, "would be the Island of Twilight?"

When they reached a point where it was no longer safe for his ship, Sinbad had a dinghy lowered and rowed up quietly to the closest solid, or mostly solid, ground. As Murshid had said, the island was actually a floating raft of debris, so tangled together that one could walk on it, as long as one walked carefully. Landing, Sinbad was glad that he'd chosen the lightest of his companions, Tishimi, Henri, and Haroun, to accompany him. One misstep might have sent Ralf or even Omar straight through to the depths of the sea below.

It was Tishimi who led the way, seeking the safest path. Henri followed, then Sinbad and Haroun, assisting Zahir and keeping the trembling old man from stumbling. The heaviest of them, Rasim came after, moving with surprising dexterity for an automaton. As for Malaika, she'd faded into mist again, appearing once in a while to readjust her path. Apparently mist could not see.

They finally reached the point where the debris was so thick there was no longer any chance of stepping through. That, however, meant the island's defenses couldn't fall through either and as far as Sinbad could see, there were defenses aplenty. The things he'd seen moving were, for the most part, all too obviously skeletons. Bodies had washed up in this dark place and though their rotting flesh could not live, one with the powers of a Puppet Master could set them moving.

Further in were larger things. Not monsters, alive or dead, but strange combinations of the debris that surrounded the sphere. A horse of broken wood, its nostrils flared; a huge childlike figure dressed in pieces of sail; a woman, tall as a house, formed from strands of seaweed, all waving behind her like so many banners. Other things moved further away, impossible to make out in the dim light.

Malaika appeared beside Sinbad. "Those were the Puppet Master's creations, his toys, created to entertain himself in his loneliness. But the usurper has surely turned them to weapons to use against us. Have a care."

Before Sinbad could ask another question, Malaika disappeared again and he had a feeling she was evading his questions and suspicions. Well enough; let them get Zahir safely healed and then they would see. In the meantime, "The dead ones seem unable to see, or hear us. Try to move past them without being touched."

They crept through the debris, Haroun gagging as one of the bodies came too close. Nor could Sinbad blame him, for that one was particularly ripe and bloated. If its belly burst as it walked, the stink would be overpowering.

The first danger came from small things. The Puppet Master had been nothing if not prolific in his creations and the giants weren't alone. Toys for children, marionettes, carved soldiers, even a spinning top, wandered around the debris, moving with obvious design, so that a passerby could hardly walk through without stumbling into one.

By ill-luck, it was Sinbad who did so. Focused on keeping Zahir moving, his foot slipped on something wet and dank. He slid sideways, kicking a spider-shaped toy that no child had any business wanting. It jumped, landing among other toys and a chain reaction followed quickly. Hundreds of toys turned and rushed towards the party.

"Run," Sinbad ordered, slinging Zahir over his shoulder. They could stand and fight and as small as their opponents were, they'd likely win, but it would take time and use valuable resources. "Spread out and get to the sphere."

The others obeyed quickly, dodging between and over the island's debris. They slid and slipped, feeling small toys strike at them and sometimes fell. Once dozens of the toys buried Henri beneath them with their bodies. Somehow the Gaul surged upwards out of the attack and rushed onwards.

Tishimi was first to one of the giant puppets, the childlike one. It swung at her, moving slowly but inexorably, and she dodged away just in time. She paused, eyeing the thing, then her sword flashed as she cut through something along the back of one of the thing's legs. As it stumbled to one knee, she repeated the maneuver on the other leg and it fell forward. A strange sound followed. Weeping, like a hurt child.

The horse came at Henri then and he was forced to shoot its eyes out. It screamed, dancing wildly in place as if in pain. Then the woman formed of plants was reaching for Sinbad and he cut at her with his scimitar. His blade sliced the thick leaves and she too cried out, still trying to grasp him. Seeing no answer but to keep cutting, though the sound of her wails were enough to break his heart, Sinbad sliced and sliced and sliced. Until, at last, there was nothing left but tattered fronds upon the ground.

They reached the sphere and found Malaika waiting for them. "Well done," she said calmly. "Come inside. Before the others find us."

The sphere's interior was a softly glowing maze of corridors. There seemed to be no order, no pattern to them and, even worse, they turned and twisted in directions that Sinbad's mind swore was impossible. At one point he was certain they were upside down. When he asked Malaika, though, all she said was, "Directions have no meaning here. Just follow me."

The little dancer led them down passage after passage until they came to a room that, fortunately for Sinbad's peace of mind, appeared completely normal. There was glass cylinder the size of a man at its center and more vats of black water surrounding it, but it had a floor, walls, and ceiling.

"Put Zahir in there," Malaika requested quietly, pointing at the cylinder. "And I will set the spell to restore him."

Sinbad started forward and was surprised when Rasim joined him. Together they settled the sorcerer inside the bottom of the cylinder and stepped back. Unsure what to expect, as the light began to swirl around the nearly unconscious man, Sinbad found himself certain that something was going wrong. When Malaika made a startled, almost frightened, sound, he knew he was right.

The light within the sphere pulsed wildly and without pattern. Its colors shifted and changed in a nauseating display. The old man's figure disintegrated to broken pieces of green rock, causing Malaika to cry out helplessly. Then lightning flared, sparking around the room and striking the vats surrounding them. Somehow it didn't surprise Sinbad when humanoid figures rose from the dark water. Their forms were blurred and indistinct, but he thought they were supposed to be armored soldiers.

At the same time, Rasim took three long steps to where Malaika stood and grasped her by the throat. More lightning crackled around his metal hand and she cried out, body flaring brilliantly as he lifted her into the air. "Move a hand, draw a blade, raise your bow, and I shatter him to the dust from which he's formed," Rasim said. "Set your weapons down and come with me."

Realizing he'd allowed Rasim's amusing personality to lull him into false security, Sinbad growled a curse but obeyed. The others, seeing no choice, did as well, with one exception. "I will not be disarmed," Tishimi growled and, before anyone could speak or move, rolled between two of their captors to freedom. "I will come for you, Captain," she shouted, disappearing through a doorway. "Keep safe until then!"

Although Rasim muttered angrily, he didn't order the soldiers guarding them to follow her. It was a failure that left Sinbad wondering, even as he, Henri and Haroun obediently, if unwillingly, allowed themselves to be led through the halls again, until they stepped out into what appeared to be brightly lit open air, high above an azure sea.

Haroun swallowed and stared. "I'm glad I'm not afraid of heights," he said, as Sinbad realized that what surrounded them was an illusion. There were walls but some power projected an image that concealed their true appearance. He could see slight lines, here and there, that revealed the square shape of the room.

At the center was a throne and somehow, Sinbad was unsurprised to find a familiar figure seated in it, his eyes squeezed tight. Heavyset and broad-shouldered, it was his old rival, Anwar abd Anwar. "Well," he said. "I suppose I should have expected this. So you're in charge, after all?"

The Clockwork Sorcerer opened his eyes and quite suddenly Rasim dropped Malaika to the floor and went still. Not that it mattered because she was too weak to do anything but lay limp and helpless. "In charge, Sinbad? Of course, I am. That's why I'm wearing manacles and rags. And we won't even talk about the fact that I haven't eaten in days, or showered, or...."

Sinbad interrupted. "You've made your point. I noticed the rags, but not the manacles, I admit." Now that Anwar mentioned them, though, they were quite obvious. As was the smell. "Bit off more than you could chew?"

"Never, Sinbad. Just a minor setback." From Anwar's expression, he didn't look as if he believed himself.

Something flickered behind Anwar. Strange flames colored a peculiar and oddly sickening shade of puce. "I am more than a minor setback, sorcerer. And now that you've accomplished the task I set you, you may be silent. Or I will end your pathetic and useless life right here."

Guessing this was the efrit that had taken the Puppet Master's place, Sinbad offered, "It seems unwise to bring your enemy straight into the center of your power."

"You? You are nothing, Sinbad. A mere human. Armed with nothing but a fast mouth, even your vaunted luck has no hope of defeating me." The flames gestured at Malaika, "That? That is just a doll created by my predecessor, a tool to help him seek my name. And now, even if he knows it, he is shattered to dust and can do nothing."

Something tugged on the back of Sinbad's leg and he felt it climb up. Not wanting Murshid to attract attention, he kept talking. "You're saying Zahir al Sa'id was the Puppet Master, after all?"

"Who else? He hid himself well behind a veil of empty eyes and empty mind, but do you truly think that," the flames indicated Malaika again, "is anything more than a vessel of his power? All it is, is a weak little doll, barely useful for anything but dancing."

Henri growled and Sinbad shared the sentiment. Still, he kept his lips curved in a smug smile as Murshid found his way to a spot just beside Sinbad's left hand. "I think she is useful for more than that," Sinbad murmured, to the efrit's obvious amusement.

Murshid slid something cool and smooth into Sinbad's hand and whispered, "Tishimi is coming. Give that and fire to Malachi."

The sound of running feet drew everyone's attention towards the only entrance and Tishimi suddenly appeared there, rolling between two of the guards. Behind her came a noise, a thudding sound that Sinbad suddenly recognized, for it was accompanied by crying. Automatically, he and the others dodged sideways, rolling across the floor. Sinbad made sure to land beside Malaika, guessing she was the one Murshid meant by Malachi.

The Puppet Master's doll, the child shaped one, came into the room, bent over so it could get through the corridor, swinging her arms wildly, knocking the efrit's soldiers down as she stumbled after Tishimi. Sinbad took advantage of the confusion to put the stone he'd been given into Malaika's hand. Then, with a prayer to Allah that he'd understood, he broke the seal on his bottle of fire and poured it out on the dancer's still body.

The heat of the flames rose only momentarily before being sucked straight down. Malaika's form flared again, but this time, her eyes opened, one blood red, the other bright green. She stared blankly at Sinbad, looking lost and confused for the longest moment. Then she floated upright towards the throne. She paused but a moment to calm the child puppet, then turned to face the enemy. "Keep his tools occupied, please."

It was Henri who demanded, a little querulously, "With what weapons?"

"Ah, yes. Those." Malaika snapped her fingers and Sinbad found his scimitar rising an inch or so from his nose. He grabbed it without complaint, guessing Malaika had more important concerns. Henri and Haroun's weapons appeared a moment later and both set to fighting the efrit's guards with a will. Tishimi, of course, was already armed and already cutting down the enemy. As for the huge doll, it sat down to watch with wide dark eyes.

It was a difficult fight but as with all the efrit's other monsters, the soldiers could still be hurt and still be killed. As before, they melted to black water, until the floor was slick with the stuff. Sinbad slid once, but Rasim, under the Clockwork Sorcerer's control and once more on Sinbad's side caught him and kept him from falling.

At the dais, Malaika and the efrit faced each other, flames flaring from one to the other. "You can't be strong enough," the efrit complained, though it was obvious she was, now. "You're just a puppet."

"Yes, I am," she agreed. "I always have been."

"Zahir created you!"

"Now that's where you're wrong. I created Zahir from my very substance. He was my child, born to leave this lonely place and seek the things I could not. His creation weakened me, and before I could recover, you came and stole my Self from me. And now he is destroyed and I will not forgive you."

That confirmed Sinbad's suspicions and he wished Malaika had trusted him enough to tell the truth. He cut down another soldier and tried to make his way to the throne. Anwar was still imprisoned there, eyes squeezed tight as he used Rasim to aid the fight.

The efrit had been momentarily silenced by Malaika's admission, but soon it was obvious that he was still the stronger. "Even at your fullest power, puppet, master of puppets, I will defeat you. You have nothing but the fires within you to battle me and I am fire itself. If only you had my name, little puppet, but that is lost with Zahir!"

Malaika faltered and Sinbad saw self-doubt suffuse her fragile features. Looking at her, though, he realized why Murshid had given him that green stone. "Malaika! Malachi! Listen to me."

"He's right." Malaika was backing away, real fear on her face. "I can't."

"You can."

"No."

"You can because your left eye is green!"

Her eyes widened and she glanced Sinbad's way. Then she rose into the air above the efrit, whose flames flared up to strike her as uselessly as hers had him. Softly, she said, "Zahir al Sa'id, flesh of my flesh, I call on you. Give me the name of the one I face, that we might end him together."

An image of another superimposed itself on Malaika. Not an old man, not now, but a pale haired youth with emerald eyes and very nearly Malaika's face. He raised a hand and spoke a single word. "μβαδίρ."

With a scream that forced Sinbad to cover his ears, the efrit flared bright, spun around once, twice and thrice. Then it was gone in a cloud of oily black smoke. Light faded from the room and when it brightened again, he was standing on the deck of the *Blue Nymph*, his crew staring at him and his companions with startled expressions.

It took Sinbad a moment to truly realize where he was, by which time the sky above them was lightening, transforming to a soft bluish-purple shade that - in his own world - heralded dawn. The water shifted as well, taking on that same color, until he felt as if he stood within a particularly lovely blue opal.

The crew stared behind Sinbad and he turned to see Malaika hanging above him, smiling a strange sad smile. Murshid sat on her shoulder like it was a throne and waving and grinning at Sinbad broadly, his third eye glowing like her right one. It took little for Sinbad to guess that he was, and always had been her tool.

"You must return home now," Malaika said. "This world needs cleansing and I have much to do."

"Is there anything you need?"

"Not that you can give, Captain. Indeed, it is I who owe you." A huge hand formed of the water itself rose up and poured several Emperor's ransoms worth of gems, scrolls and gold on the *Blue Nymph's* deck. Only Omar's sharp order kept the crew from moving towards it and Malaika chuckled, "Don't be greedy. There is more than enough for all, I think."

She turned her attention on Anwar, who sat grumpily on the deck, his automaton silent beside him. Thoughtfully, she said, "You betrayed me."

"It isn't as if I was given a choice," the Clockwork Sorcerer protested. "That efrit of yours captured me and tortured me."

"He wasn't my efrit and I seem to remember telling you to keep out of this. You were to get Murshid to Sinbad and hide, not go seeking the Sea of Night yourself."

"And not learn the truth of what you and Zahir were? How could I leave it alone?"

She shook her head. "One day that curiosity of yours will be the end of you. Are you satisfied with what you've gained?"

"I... think so."

"Then go home, Anwar, who serves himself, and don't come here again. There is nothing else I have to offer you." She waved her hand and the sorcerer's gryphon appeared out of nowhere.

Sulkily, Anwar climbed onto his mount's back. With a glare at Sinbad, he said, "We'll meet again, I promise. Until then, remember what I said about those knots." Then, his gryphon took off, catching hold of his automaton and they disappeared.

Malaika had a few private words for Henri and, to Sinbad's surprise, Tishimi and Ralf. Then she beckoned Sinbad. "I cannot ask you to stay," she told him quietly. "This is not a world for you. Nor can I leave it again. It wouldn't be safe."

Something in her eyes spoke of loneliness and Sinbad offered the only thing he could. "Those puppets of yours aren't just toys. Anymore than you are." She smiled wanly and he added, "There's nothing to stop you from recreating Zahir. There was enough of him left to know that efrit's name. Perhaps there's enough to remember the rest."

"I would could I be so certain. If I do, it shall have to be with far more care, lest I am once more cast from my throne." She drifted down to kiss Sinbad's cheek, then held out her hands, holding out a gem on a silver chain; as blue as the bluest sky, as clear as the purest water. "All I can do is give you this."

"It's beautiful, but you did just give the whole crew more jewels than we know what to do with."

"This one is special, Sinbad. It will protect its wearer from magical attacks. It is not all powerful, nor will it withstand everything, but it can give you time. And sometimes time is all you need."

Sinbad eyed the thing. "It's awfully large," he said. "Not that I'm complaining, but…."

"It's not for you, you foolish adventurer. It's for the one you love most. Give it to her, with my thanks." Before Sinbad could ask Malaika's meaning, she floated backwards and everything around the ship dimmed. A moment later they once more sailed on the azure sea of their own world, the late afternoon sun shining bright upon them.

Sinbad pondered the jewel in his hand for several minutes, trying to understand Malaika's meaning. Then, smiling broadly, he hung the chain around the neck of his most and best beloved. Who else could it be, after all, but the *Blue Nymph* herself.

Then he turned and eyed his crew, clapping his hands together. "All right, you lowlifes! There's treasure to count and a ship to return to port! Get to work!"

Behind him, the *Blue Nymph's* figurehead raised wooden hands to clasp the gemstone close, a secret smile on her face as the ship bounced and danced happily upon the waves.

The End

Voyaging with Sinbad

When I was a youngster, "The Golden Voyage of Sinbad" was one of my many much-loved movies. It had strange lands, powerful magic, adventure, swordplay and monsters. It also had Tom Baker as the villain. I admit without shame to having liked him better than the king he'd cursed. It never hit me until long after I'd watched "Doctor Who" that he was the 4th Doctor, but I can be slow that way.

Several of the scenes in "Golden Voyage" stayed with me all my life. The ship's figurehead battling Sinbad, having ripped herself free of her prow. The Hindu Goddess statue dancing death under Prince Koura's command. And, of course, that moment of strange joy when the evil Prince creates a homunculus and watches it explore its world like a proud father.

The other two Harryhausen movies were great fun, but "Golden Voyage" struck deepest and when Ron made a call for a Sinbad tale for this anthology, I jumped at the chance. And that, of course, meant that I had no choice but to include an homage to the things I'd loved in that particular movie. References are, quite obviously, scattered throughout the story.

Having decided to do a Sinbad story, I needed to get a feel for the milieu and that meant reading at least one previous volume, if not more. Definitely, must read more! I'd a couple of ideas floating around, one of which didn't fit well enough (yet) and the other…well, let's just say I had a moment of panic when the description of I.A. Watson's story described a situation similar to what I'd been contemplating.

To my great relief, it wasn't the same. It did, however, have a character I could use; Anwar abd Anwar, Anwar who serves Anwar, the Clockwork Sorcerer. The fellow could be anything. In my mind, he's an expy of Prince Koura, though Ian may well scoff at that thought. I wasn't sure if Ian has any use for him later, of course, so I didn't want to go too far with him in any direction, but he could be an excellent bait to drag Sinbad into his adventure.

Another influence on the story comes from the old Liavek series. The magic is different as is the world and its Gods, but the Arabian Nights feel is very strong. I created the Inn of the Seven Stars with that thought in mind, it's a place that doesn't affect the story directly, but hopefully, it sets the tone. If I write more Sinbad stories, it, and its mysterious proprietress may well appear again.

For those wondering what, exactly, Malaika is, I would I could answer that. So does she. Perhaps, one day, we'll both know. In the meantime, there are more adventures, more magic and more swordplay to be had and I hope you'll have fun with it!

BARBARA DORAN - has been making up stories for as long as she can remember. From playing Ms. Marvel to her best friend's Captain Marvel to writing new stories for old characters (Hannibal King, X-Men, Green Hornet, The Saint, The Shadow and many others), to writing gaming and anime fanfiction online.

After ten years behind the keyboard as a software engineer, Barbara realized that her true love wasn't coding but making stuff up. So when she left that career in favor of dealing with two frequent interruptions of her life (namely her own personal Tiger and Dragon), she decided to use what little time they allowed her to work on writing. Her Long Suffering Husband, without whom she could never have managed such a goal, has been nothing if not supportive.

Along with reading every mystery, SF and fantasy book she could get her hands on, Barbara grew up watching Star Trek, Batman, Green Hornet, along with the usual Saturday morning cartoons. She became addicted to shows like Battle of the Planets and Doctor Who in her teens and discovered Run Run Shaw's martial arts flicks some years later. Those influences, along with a love of folklore and mythology, have become part of the world, some small portion of her mind lives in. When, of course, she isn't chasing Tiger and Dragon from one school event to another.

Barbara can be contacted at <BarbaraDoran@sumergoscriptum.com>. Her website is <http://www.sumergoscriptum.com/barbaradoran/>.

THE DESERT CONTEST

By Ron Fortier

So, while Sinbad El Ari and his three companions, Omar, Rafi and Haroun were off on a secret mission for the Caliph of Baghdad, others of the *Blue Nymph's* fearsome crew were having their own misadventures.

The twenty blue-clad horsemen crested a giant sand dune and looked upon the oasis camp that was their destination. They could see Bedouin herders tending their camels and women moved in and out of the dozens of tents carrying out their daily chores. The leader of the horsemen nodded to his men, waved his hand forward and spurred his beautiful black stallion forward.

Screaming at the top of their lungs, the desert riders galloped down the loose sands and charged boldly into the middle of the camp causing people to scamper out of their way hurriedly. As one, they halted directly in front of the largest tent; one festooned with colored ribbons and flying a pennant with the image of a crescent star on it.

Having heard the ruckus commotion, a figure emerged from the open entrance to the tent. He was a sturdy fellow with a big belly, a trimmed brown beard and his clothing was of the richest silks and fabrics. Centered on his turban was a bright red ruby the size of a robin's egg. Upon seeing the horsemen, he bowed slightly, touched his right hand to his head and his lips and then opened his arms in welcome. "Salaam, it is good to see you, Abu Sha."

The tall, imposing horseman peeled back his indigo blue scarf and revealed a handsome, youthful visage of a dusky hue with dark brown eyes and a neat mustache and goatee. He chuckled, threw one leg over his cantle and dropped off his horse gracefully.

"It is good to see you as well, my brother," Abu Sha loudly proclaimed as he hugged his older sibling and they kissed each other's cheeks. "You grow larger with each passing year, Turan Bey," he said slapping the Sheik's stomach.

"What can I say, Allah gave me a passion for good food and wine," the big man retorted. "I am slave to all delicacies of the flesh."

And with that, Sheik Ali Turan Bey waved his brother and his men to join him in the coolness of his massive pavilion. "Come, refresh yourselves with some of that very sustenance. My wives have prepared a wondrous feast in anticipation of your arrival."

As the brothers escaped the brutal midday heat for the relief of the open-air enclosure, Abu Sha marveled at the luxurious surroundings Turan Bey traveled in. The sand floor was covered with thick rugs and colorful, fluffy pillows were scattered about for sitting and reclining. All the desert sheik had to do was clap his hands and several lovely harem girls materialized with platters of roasted lamb and goblets of sweet red wine. It was only natural that Abu Sha felt a twinge of envy towards the brother. Then again, being the older, he had rightly inherited their father's wealth and position upon his death. Abu Sha was left with a small portion of his father's livestock which included several dozen camels and six of the most magnificent Arabian horses ever to race across the arid wastelands.

The brothers were merchants by trade and worked well together. Turan Bey had a head for numbers and knew how to haggle with neighboring tribes, whereas Abu Sha loved nothing more than leading a long-distance caravan to carry their goods to and from the ports that dotted the coastline; Baghdad being the most profitable.

In fact, the brothers only had one thing in common; their desire to outdo the other no matter the contest.

"So, I take it you have recruited a new champion for the Warriors Challenge," the Sheik prodded his younger brother as they settled down on the pile of cushions to make themselves comfortable.

"Your concern is most kind," Abu Sha said. "But you needn't worry about me, brother."

"Does that mean you still haven't found a champion?" A sly smile played over Turan Bey's chubby face. "I'm told that our fellow tribesmen are even now trekking their way here through the desert, each bringing with them their strongest and most accomplished fighter."

"There is still three more days before the rise of the full moon," Abu Sha declared. "And I'm sure by now my agent, Bezi Akbar, has found the greatest fighter in all the land."

The Sheik was about to say something else when a giant of a bald-headed black man entered the tent from the back side carrying a tray upon which were set a goblet and two expensive cups of beaten silver. He was dressed in pointed slippers, baggy pantaloons, and a simple leather vest that showed off his massive torso and powerful physique. He set these down before the two brothers, then took several steps backward and folded his powerful arms over his burly chest.

"I certainly hope he services better than he did last year," Turan Bey chided as he picked up the goblet and began to pour red wine into the cups. He nodded his head towards his silent slave. "It's been so long since anyone has given poor Molani a real challenge. How long did your last fellow…ah…the sailor from Kush…last? What was it, all of five minutes before Molani tossed him out of the tent onto his backside."

Abu Sha took the offered drink from his chortling brother and did his best to hide his anger and frustration. In the five years since Turan Bey had started the annual martial arts tournament, he had won every single one thanks to the giant African. And every year Abu Sha was humiliated watching his own champions easily defeated. He was beginning to think there was no one who could defeat the mighty black warrior.

Still, his agent, Bezi Akbar, realized what would befall him if he failed to find a warrior capable of beating the powerful Molani. Abu Sha relied on that fear to propel Akbar to succeed …or else face the consequences. If he lost to his inflated brother one more time, somebody was going to die.

The tavern was called the Shark's Teeth and was located in the dock district so as to service the hundreds of sailors, both native and foreign, who made their living on the high seas. Of course much of the goods that were unloaded from the magnificent ships eventually found its way throughout the land via the caravans of the various desert dwellers. Thus on any given night, the local watering hole was packed with both seamen and Bedouins, all out to have a good time in between their sea voyages and treks through the arid wastelands.

It was here Henri Delacrois, Ralf Gunarson and Tishimi Osara came to wet their parched throats and escape from the boredom of being land bound while the *Blue Nymph* was being refitted. Finding an empty table at the inn's far wall from the entrance, only because its previous occupants had all passed out from too much wine and been dragged into the alley behind the place, the trio ordered their individual drinks from one of the four barmaids who wove in and out of the boisterous crowd. Three of the four were daughters of the proprietor, Hassan, while the fourth was a close cousin.

"Now there's a fine looking damsel," Delacrois commented twisting one end of his mustache as the well shaped girl left to go get their drinks from the bar. He'd set his bow and quiver against the wall behind them and now stretched back on the hard wooden stool that were the only chairs in the place. Hassan made his profit selling food and drink, not luxurious furniture.

"Ho, here we go again," Gunarson chuckled giving Tishimi a slight wink. "How long do you think it will take him this time?"

"Heh, how long will what take me? You blonde barbarian."

"For you to get into a fight over that wench."

"Sir, you do me a grave injustice," Delacrois feigned a sad expression. "Is it my fault I have a weakness for the fairer sex?"

"What you have is an incorrigible talent for always getting us into trouble," Tishimi spoke up, her hands folded together on the table. "Just once it would be nice for the three of us to have a friendly drink without it resulting in a demeaning barroom brawl."

Delacrois was about to offer up another retort when he was interrupted by the sounds of drums and flutes. Everyone in the tavern quieted and turned their attention to a curtain hanging over the entrance to the building's back rooms. Seated to either side of these brightly dyed drapes were the musicians eagerly playing their rhythmic tune. It was a familiar melody most of the patrons recognized immediately and a series of boisterous cheers went up along with a smattering of applause.

"Hmm, so what have we here?" the Gaul queried with a smirk on his face.

The curtains parted and out onto the main floor stepped a woman dressed in veils with long, lustrous brown hair and rings on her fingers and toes. As she moved gracefully between the tables, her raised arms angulated like twin snakes and her entire body seemed to move with the music in a sensuous pattern. Then, while making a gliding pirouette, the dancer peeled away two of her veils to expose her tanned belly in which a bright red ruby had been set in her navel.

"Yasmina!" several voices cried at the woman's appearance thus identifying her to the trio from the *Blue Nymph*.

At the same time, the drummers began to slap their leather topped kettles increasing the tempo of their music. The woman's movement kept time and as her body gyrated and her stomach muscles began to vibrate quicker and quicker with each new step her feet took.

"Ah, now that's more like it," Delacrois declared, his eyes following the shaking form of the belly-dancer as she made her way through the room. The barmaid returned with their drinks, three mugs of spiced wine, and set them on the table. The big Viking tossed her several dinars which he stuffed in her apron pocket before disappearing.

Gunarson downed half his drink before coming up for air. "Not as good as mead but it will do well enough," he grinned. Seeing his companion had yet to touch his drink, he slapped the Gaul on the arm. "Drink up, Henri, I plan on drinking you under the table before this night is over."

"What?" The handsome Frenchmen momentarily took his eyes from the beautiful Yasmina and looked down at the cup before him. "Oui, of course." He picked it up and turned his gaze back to the veiled entertainer as he drank. Gunarson looked at Tishimi, holding her own mug in her hands and both of them laughed aloud. Seeing their friend mesmerized by an alluring female was all too familiar to them.

Just then, a tall, bearded Arab wearing a blue turban, called out to the sensual dancer as she neared his table. "Come here, my desert flower, and shower me with your womanly delights." The four men seated with him all laughed and urged him on enough so that as the raven haired beauty attempted to slide around their table, the loudmouth Arab reached out and tried to grab her.

At first, Yasmina was amused and waved her hands out towards his face as she moved away from him. But not to be repulsed, the drunken patron would not so easily be put off and he rose up out of his chair and lunged for her. Wrapping his arms around her body, he tried to pull her to him. The dancer, taken by surprise, tried to fend him off but he was too strong for her. She begged him to release her but he thought she was merely teasing him and he tightened his hold on her.

"Oh, no, my desert flower, Hiran will not set you free until he has tasted the honey of your lips." With that, he pulled the veil from her lower face.

For the most part, the rest of the tavern patrons had been amused by the Arab's antics but when the veil was torn from Yasmina's face, revealing a dusky visage of elegant beauty, silence fell on the room.

"Unhand the lady, you oafish pig!" Henri Delacrois demanded as he stood up and yelled at the Arab holding his fleshly prize.

Hiran, the Arab, turned to see who it was that insulted him. The sight of the Gaulish archer was not what he had expected to see. Still, the foreigner was smaller by a foot and the desert warrior was not about to suffer public humiliation at the hands of such a fool. He let the girl go and from the black sash about his middle, whipped out a curved three-foot scimitar.

"You dare call me a pig, you uncouth, foreign dog," he retorted as she began to push through the tables, his sword high over his head. "I will teach you some manners while I cut out that foolish tongue of yours."

Delacrois stood his ground and when Hiran was close enough to wield his weapon, the wiry Gaul ducked under the sharp blade while extending his left leg. Unable to stop his forward momentum, the angry Arab tripped over the leg and barreled head first into the back wall. There was a loud smack when his head, cushioned by his turban, made contact with the unmoving wall and Hiran dropped senseless to the floor.

"So much for that lout," Delacrois smiled at his friends as he brushed his hands together.

"My hero," Yasmina praised as she started for the handsome rogue. Sadly before she could reach her dashing savior, Hiran's oafish brother, Ralule got up from his table and threw his mug at Delacrois. It caught the archer on the temple and smashed into a thousand pieces. Suddenly Delacrois was seeing stars as he fell onto his back. At which point Ralule rushed forward prepared to inflict more bodily harm to the fellow who had humiliated his brother.

At this point both Ralf Gunarson and Tishimi Osara hastily finished their drinks and got to their feet ready to do battle. Like it or not, their mate had once again instigated another brawl they were honor bound to enter. Of course, the truth was neither had ever shied away from a good fight. That was evident when Gunarson shot out his massive right arm so as to collide with the big Ralule as he raced by. The blow knocked the Arab off his feet and into the air. He sailed some ten feet before crashing onto a table spilling the drinks of a half dozen sailors before breaking the table. Shouting curses, all six burly seaman began swinging and punching anyone close enough to hit.

At this, Gunarson laughed heartily, turned, grabbed his own table and picked it up as if it was a weightless disc. He spun around and threw it into the center of the melee knocking over a group of men like bowling pins.

Seeing this, a group of Bedouins converged on the powerful Viking and swarmed over him swinging chairs, mugs and anything else they could find. For a second the blonde headed Norseman was buried under a pile of robe-wearing fighters. Then he gave out a mighty roar and shot up from the floor, his tree-sized arms flailing around wildly. Each fist hitting Bedouins and felling them like a hammer driving a nail. Seeing the young man joyously battling overwhelming odds was truly a remarkable sight for those lucky enough to be far way from those swinging blows.

Such a witness, seated in the alcove by the front entrance, was Bezi Akbar; Turon Bey's agent. He'd been seated by himself trying to drown his woes in wine due to his failure to find any real fighters of worth to recruit for his master. Then, as if Allah had magically answered his prayers, the three outworlders had arrived and within minutes, he was witnessing one of the most impressive feats of martial acumen he had ever seen. Truly this blonde savage was exactly the kind of champion he had been sent to find.

Bezi Akbar couldn't believe his good fortune. Then suddenly one of the combatants came flying through the air straight for his table. He dove to the wooden floor just as the man crashed into his booth. Apparently despite his turn of luck, it was obvious he still had to remain alert as more of the tavern's patrons were quickly joining the fracas until it wasn't safe to raise one's head above knee level. Now men of various ships were fighting sailors from other ships while the Bedouins who belonged to different tribes were going at one another. All the while the blonde Viking was laughing loudly as he continued to drop any opponent foolish enough to come within range of his fists.

On hands and knees, Bezi Akbar made his way through the thick forest of legs before him and finally managed to reach what he hoped was safety behind the main bar. Here he found Hassan the owner, and his daughters, huddled together while chaos ruled on the other side of the counter.

Bezi nodded politely to Hassan and gladly accepted the gourd of wine the shopkeeper offered him.

"And to think I gave up a profitable career as a camel breeder to open up this cursed establishment in this hellhole of a town," Hassan cursed as several mugs crashed into the shelves behind them smashing more bottles of expensive liquor.

"It is not a fair world," Bezi agreed, wiping his mouth after taking a long swallow. "All must suffer at times."

Just then a roar went up amongst the crowd followed by a moment of silence. His curiosity getting the best of him, Abu Sha's agent grabbed the counter and pulled his head up to see what had transpired to end the fighting. He was just in time to see the big Viking drop onto several men, while an Arab stood on one of the remaining tables still intact holding a broken chair in his hands; a chair he had just used to knock down the mighty brawler.

"I did it!" the fellow cried out in triumph. "I, Koomar El By, have defeated the yellow haired giant."

For a second the crowd just stood looking from the boasting Arab to the now comatose Viking stretched atop several of their other brethren. Then, before they could react one way or another, there was an ear-piercing cry and a small black figure jumped up onto the table to confront the gloating Koomar El By.

It was a small, black-clad Oriental woman with the short dark hair. Bezi Akbar remembered her as being one of the Viking's drinking companions. Now she stood before the Arab calmly sizing him up.

Then, like a cobra striking, her right hand shot out and hit him in the stomach. Woof! The air expelled from the Arab's lungs as he doubled over in pain, only to meet Tishimi Osara's knee with his face. There was a loud smack and he was driven back off the table but not before he let go of the broken pieces of the chair he had used as a weapon. Tishimi caught them and immediately wove these sticks in front of her in a rapid series of thrusts and parries. She was completing a bow-stick kata; a formalized set of moves she had mastered long ago in her native Japan.

All watched in fascination until she came to an abrupt stop, both chair legs in front of her in an X position. Then she looked at the assembly of maddened men below and a strange gleam appeared in her eyes. She gave out another high-pitched cry and launched herself into the air.

Before she hit the floor, both her legs snapped out connecting with two turbaned heads. Then her improvised weapons struck and another two fighters joined the first pair on the floor.

Their reverie broken, one of the sailors bellowed, "GET HER!"

But that was easier said then done, as the female martial artist became a blur of punches and kicks too fast for any eye to follow. And although she was the smallest combatant in the tightly packed room, it was this closeness that impeded those around her as he had no real space to maneuver whereas she twisted and danced evading every single attack. Most she parried while at the same time continuing to inflict her deadly strikes, none of which failed to miss a target. Jaws were crushed, heads knocked silly and legs swept away to drop confused battlers. Fighting the whirling mistress of destruction was an impossibility as all soon learned and within a matter of minutes, the entire floor of the tavern was littered with moaning men.

Standing completely unscathed in their midst, Tishimi Osara took a deep breath, and then stepping over her defeated opponents, marched to the bar and there put down her weapons. She spotted Bezi Akbar, his eyes wide with amazement at what he had just beheld. His mind was having a hard time reconciling what he had seen. This diminutive woman had bested over two dozen men...all by herself!

Impossible! And yet he had seen it.

"Could I please have something to drink?" Tishimi asked him. "I am very thirsty."

Bezi jumped up and grabbed one of the few unbroken bottles from the smashed shelf behind him. As he did so, Hassan and his daughters slowly got to their feet and for the first time surveyed the damage done to their tavern.

"By Allah's holy beard," Hassan gasped. "I am ruined. Look what these barbarians have done to my establishment."

"Calm down," Bezi Akbar said as he uncorked the wine bottle and handed it to Tishimi. "For the opportunity to have beheld such a contest of fighting prowess, I am only to happy to reimburse you for the damages."

"Thank you," Tishimi smiled and took a long swallow of the sweet red wine.

"You will?" Hassan looked at desert Arab with mild confusion, unsure he had heard him correctly.

Bezi Akbar dug into his tunic, grabbed hold of a small leather pouch and pulling it out handed it over to the astonished Hassan. "Here, there should be more than enough dinars in there to buy you twice as many tables and chairs...and whatever else you require to repair this poor excuse for a watering hole."

Happy to have the money, Hassan ignored Bezi's insult. "Oh, thank you, young master. May Allah bless you to the end of your days. If there is anything either I, or my lovely daughters, can do to make your stay in our town more pleasant, you have but to ask."

Bezi Akbar started to say something when there was a commotion in the middle of the room, now littered with comatose men and mountains of broken furniture. From one such pile, a handsome, bearded blonde head emerged.

"Who is the cowardly dog who struck me from behind?" roared a very irate Ralf Gunarson. As he climbed to his feet, he delicately massaged the goose-egg on the back of his skull. "I will tear the villain's limbs off one at a time. Ow."

"Oh, thank you, young master."

"Easy, old friend," Tishimi got his attention and waved her bottle to indicate the scene before the Norseman. "He's been dealt with and I doubt seriously you could find him amongst that heap."

Gunarson shrugged and walked over to the bar to join his friend. "Perhaps. Ah, but it was a good fight. I enjoyed it greatly."

Tishimi passed him the bottle and he took a long swig. Putting it down, he looked at Bezi Akbar and Hassan. "Fighting makes me hungry. What do you have to eat in this place?"

"Ah, the kitchen is in the back amongst the rooms we let to overnight guests," Hassan explained. "I'm sure my daughters can get you something to eat."

"But not here," Bezi Akbar saw his chance to get the two foreigners alone. "Show us to an empty room where these stout warriors may relax enjoy and such a meal in privacy."

"Of course," Hassan agreed. He turned to the same girl who had first waited on the three sailors from the *Blue Nymph*. "Kaila, show our guests to the large room by the back yard."

"Wait," Gunarson held up a hand. "What about Henri?"

"Oh, I believe he is in good hands," Tishimi said and nodded to the far wall by the curtains. There the lovely belly-dancer was seated on the floor and had the Gaul's head in her lap. He was still knocked out, but she continued to rain down kisses on his face while calling him her gallant paladin.

Gunarson and Tishimi started laughing. Even when unconscious, their companion always seemed to end up with a beautiful woman.

Sunlight poked through the light cotton drapes hitting Henri Delacrois in the face as he floated on a cloud of dreams. Scrunching his eyes, he raised an arm to block the offending light and rolled onto his side where, through several blinks, he observed a very round mountain the color of dark desert sand. It curved upward like a melon and was crowned by a dark brown nipple. The Gaul blinked again, allowing his vision to clear properly and saw that he'd left one dream for another. This one was being the twin succulent breasts of the naked Yasmina. Raising himself up onto an elbow, the rested archer ran a hand over his face and looked down on the sleeping beauty with a roguish smile as he recalled their arduous lovemaking throughout the night.

Ah, the simple pleasures of life are always the most enjoyable; he reflected watching her sleep, the silk sheet covering her from the waist down. What a night it had been; one he would not soon forget.

Still, with the coming of dawn, it was time he was rejoining his mates. Carefully, so as not to awaken Yasmina, Delacrois slid out of her bed, found his clothing on a nearby stool and quickly put on his leggings and boots. Behind the stool were his longbow and quiver of arrows along with his belt and knives. Carrying these and his remaining clothing, he made his way out of the apartment and into the corridor beyond. Here he found several of Hassan's daughters hustling about in fulfilling whatever daily chores they had. As he stuffed his arms into his tunic, Delacrois managed to find his way to the main tavern.

Here he saw several men in the process of either repairing broken furniture or merely carrying pieces outside and tossing them into a heap for later burning. Hassan was behind the bar directing a carpenter on how to rebuild his damaged liquor cabinet as the Gaul grabbed a stool and sat down.

"*Bon jour, mon ami,*" he greeted, setting his vest, quiver and bow on the bar. "Might I trouble you for something to eat? I am famished."

Hassan nodded, bent over and from under bar removed a platter with a block of cheese and several pieces of flatbread. "It's all I have right now. It will be a while before my daughters can clean up the kitchen and prepare today's meals."

"That is most sufficient," Delacrois thanked him, ripping off a piece of bread. "So, where are my two friends?" he asked as he began chewing on the bitter morsel.

He failed to notice the change in the barkeeper's eyes as the man looked about nervously before replying. "Ah, they are gone," he said finally. "They left early right after sunrise."

"Hmm, that is strange," Delacrois took one of his sharp knives and cut off a piece of white goat cheese. "It is not like them to go on without me."

"Maybe they had to be somewhere and did not want to be late," suggested Hassan, now using an old rag to clean the counter's surface. "Or maybe they just went back to your ship and await you there right now."

"Hmm, perhaps." Delacrois started to take another piece of bread. "Can I have some water with this? It's very good, but dry."

"Of course. I'll get you a jug from the back."

No sooner had Hassan disappeared behind the curtains that led to the kitchen then Delacrois heard someone calling him softly. He looked to the opposite end of the bar to see the maid Kaila standing by the corridor entrance beckoning to him urgently.

Puzzled, he left his stool and went to her. *"Bon jour, ma belle, is there some..."*

"He's lying to you," the girl blurted out interrupting him.

"What?"

"My father, he's lying to you. Your two friends didn't leave of their own accord. They were kidnapped and taken away by a desert Arab calling himself Bezi Akbar."

"Mon Dieu," the archer gasped. He shook his head, trying to reason what it was he was being told. None of it made any sense. "This is madness. Why would anyone kidnap my friends?"

"You do not believe me?" the girl questioned.

"I don't know...it's too incredible."

She grabbed his hand. "Then come with me and I will show you I am telling the truth." Reluctantly, Delacrois allowed her to pull him down the hall and around a corner. She led him to a door and pointed to it.

"This is a storage closet my father keeps his supplies in," she said. "Open it and you will see for with own eyes."

Having no idea what he would find, Delacrois took hold of the wooden handle and pulled the door wide. Light from the corridor spilled into the small, square room where he saw many barrels and crates. As his eyes adjusted to the interior's gloom he recognized Ralf Gunarson's battle-axe and broadsword along with all of Tishimi's blades piled atop one of the crates.

"Would your friends have gone off without their weapons?" Kaila asked pointing at the deadly armament. "My father took them as payment for his part in aiding Bezi Akbar to trick your friends. He gave the Arab a potion to slip into their wine that put them to sleep."

Delacrois turned on the girl, anger beginning to rise up within him. "Then what happened?"

"Once the big Viking and the warrior woman were unconscious, the Arab recruited a handful of Bedouins amongst those still in the tavern to help bind your friends with strong chains and carry them away."

"Where did he take them?"

"I don't know, sir."

Delacrois took a deep breath and tried to think but his emotions were getting the best of him. Slowly he realized he had but one course of action. He stepped into the closet, grabbed one of Tishimi's short swords and then exited.

"Let us go talk to your father," he said and walked off towards the bar, the blade held loosely by his side.

It was the hard jostling that finally awoke Tishimi Osara. She felt the heat of the harsh sun next and slowly opened her eyes. It took only seconds to understand her moving surroundings. She was on her side in the back of a small, two-wheel cart being pulled by animals beyond her line of sight though she could see the back of an Arab seated on a wooden perch. From the gait, she guessed he was driving one or two horses. Straw had been scattered on the bed of the cart and both her hands and legs were trapped in iron manacles. The cart was traveling through a featureless desert. Over her head was a cloth canopy keeping out most of the brutal rays of the sun from beating down on her...and Ralf Gunarson who was lying opposite her, his frosty blue eyes watching her.

She felt a wave of dizziness and for second tasted bile at the back of her throat and she gasped.

"Easy, little one," Gunarson cautioned. "You are feeling the last dregs of whatever it was we were given to render us senseless."

Tishimi took a long, slow breath and nodded. Opening her eyes again, she saw that the Viking's own brawny wrists and ankles were shackled like her own. "Who did this to us?"

"I'm afraid I am the villain," Bezi Akbar replied from atop his black horse as he rode up behind the small cart in time to hear her query. Tishimi lifted her head slightly and could see at least four other Bedouins riding along with the treacherous Arab.

She looked at the man and remembered his exaggerated camaraderie back in the tavern. It had all been a ploy to make them drop their guard.

"Why?" she asked bluntly. "Where are you taking us and for what purpose?"

"Ah, yes, the purpose of this unfortunate action." Bezi Akbar actually looked remorseful as he began to explain his true mission in the port town. "I am but the humble servant of the great desert sheik, Abu Sha, and it was he who commissioned me to find the best fighters in all the land for the Contest of Champions."

For the next ten minutes, the wily Arab explained the history of the martial arts gathering and how each year his master lost to his slovenly, oafish older sibling, Sheik Turon Bey. When he was finished, he lifted his right hand from the canticle of his leather saddle in a flourish. "And so you see, upon seeing the two of you easily best thirty men, it was only logical that I ....ah...take you back with me to fight for my master."

Keeping her own anger in check, Tishimi forced herself to sit up in the cart and held out her arms and displayed the crude manacles. "Why did you simply not ask us to come and fight in your contest rather than trick us in such a despicable manner? Have you no honor?"

Bezi Akbar lowered his eyes for a second. "Allah forgive me, but you are correct. I am a lowly, conniving snake. But let me ask you this, dear lady. Had I asked you and the big one to come and participate of your own free will, would you have agreed to do so?"

Tishimi couldn't lie, despite their situation. She looked at Ralph Gunarson and he smiled, pushing himself up as well to face their captor.

"No," he replied for the two of them. "We are not mercenaries who fight at another's commands. Even with these chains, Tishimi and I will not fight for your master, no matter what you do."

"Then, my giant one, you will both die."

Six hours later a lone rider, pulling a packhorse behind him, followed the wheel tracks made by Bezi Akbar's cart. Henri Delacrois was garbed in traditional Bedouin clothing, a cloth mask covered the lower part of his face as he kept his eyes on the twin grooves in the sand that seemed to go on forever.

Delacrois hated the desert; it being nothing like the lush green fields and rolling hills of Gaul where he has been raised. There the countryside was connected by old Roman stone roads that made it possible to travel from one hamlet to another with relative ease and safety. Here, in this desolate, arid land, there were no trees, river valleys or other such markers to tell one parcel of terrain from another. Everything was just sand and more sand everywhere one looked.

As he kept his horse moving along, he thought back to how he'd come very close to gutting the treacherous tavern owner, Hassan, who had aided in the capture of his companions. With Tishimi's short blade against the tavern owner's throat, the angry archer had forced him to confess his duplicity and tell him where his friends were being taken. Like a ruptured bag of beans, the frightened Hassan had spilled everything to include what he knew of the so-called Contest of Champions and how the desert Arab had kidnapped Gunarson and Tishimi to fulfill his master's orders.

As incredible as it all sounded, Delacrois had experienced so many amazing adventures as a member of Sinbad's crew, he saw this new affair as just another such perilous event. Still, he was determined to race after the others and rescue them....or die in the attempt. It was what shipmates did for one another. Had their roles been reversed and it was he who had been abducted, he knew both the young Viking and the oriental hellcat would do the same for him.

Eventually, he released Hassan and when he saw the man give his daughter, Kaila, an ugly glance, Delacrois immediately slapped the oaf across the face and warned him that upon his return, should he learn that Hassan had in any way harmed his lovely daughter, he would cut off the bar keeper's manhood and hang it on the tavern's sign over the front door. Hassan, blinking rapidly, nodded his understanding of the threat and promised he wouldn't touch the girl.

Satisfied the man was too cowardly to do anything but obey his directive, Delacrois once again sought the girl's assistance in obtaining proper Bedouin clothing and two good horses for his journey; the second would be used to carry his friend's weapons and extra water bags. A short while later he was dressed and ready to depart. Before climbing onto the chestnut brown horse, Delacrois reached into his tunic and took out a small pouch of dinars which he handed the surprised Kaila.

"For your help, I won't forget this, mademoiselle."

The girl, taken with his chivalry and generosity, lunged forward and planted a kiss on the Gaul's face. Then before he could say another word, she vanished back into the tavern. Delacrois had smiled, grabbed the reins of the pack animal and mounted his own horse. Minutes later he was riding over the hills outside of the port town and headed out into the vast, yellow desert.

And here he was miles later still keeping up with the tracks to the small cart that was carrying his friends into unknown perils. Delacrois hoped he would be in time to save them. He took a sip from one of the water bags, then he dismounted and poured some into the palm of his hand and let his horse drink. He repeated the gesture for the second horse and then got under way again while above the red orb of the sun continued to beat down on the world.

The sky was turning a majestic orange and purple when Bezi Akbar's party crested the small hill to look down on the oasis at Desarea. From the back of the wooden cart Ralf Gunarson and Tishimi Osara looked upon the massive encampment that covered the well-traveled watering spot. Desarea was well known as it boasted not one, but two deep fresh water wells at either end of its half mile locale, most of which was shaded by three dozen tall palm trees all of which sprouted huge green leaves.

"We have arrived," Bezi Akbar announced sweeping his hand towards the massive gathering.

"Who are all those people?" Tishimi inquired, her natural curiosity getting the best of her. "Or is this a typical caravan watering station?"

"Hardly," their captor resplied. "Although this is one of the most traveled oasis in all the desert. No, what you see before you are respresentives of all the major tribes come to participate in the contest with their champions."

"It reminds me of the festival of Odin," Gunarson said. "Every year before winter solstice, tribes from throughout the north countries come together to celebrate the Fall harvest and their warriors test their skills against others in various contests from hammer throwing to log-rolling. It is a joyous occasion that all relish before the coming of the long cold nights."

At this Bezi Akbar nodded. "So, we are not that different after all, Viking."

"Only in that such contests are for free men and no one is enslaved to participate in them."

Stung by Gunarson's words, the desert Arab turned away from him and shouted at the cart driver. "Move along! I've to report to my master and then we can get a decent meal and something to drink."

The driver snapped the reins and the horses started down the hill, their hooves stepping carefully in the shifting sands.

In the back of the cart, Tishimi continued to study the spread out camp familiarizing herself with its layout. Without turning her gaze from it, she whispered to Gunarson. "Try to control your temper, my friend. We must bide our time until an opportunity presents itself for us to escape."

The blonde giant leaned closer and also whispered. "Easy for you to say." He held up his fettered hands. "I will be no man's slave."

"Fine, but try not to be a fool either." Tishimi turned and locked eyes with the younger Gunarson. "It will require both our brains and muscles if we are to free ourselves...and take retribution on these black-hearted Arabs."

A cold smile appeared on the Viking's bearded face. "Ah, now that's more to my liking."

As the big man leaned back against the wall of the cart, Tishimi returned to her studying of the camp now closer still. She also said a few silent prayers that her friend's impetuous nature wouldn't get them killed before she could plan their escape.

If the camp looked like a small village, by the time they were rolling through its center, Tishimi adjusted her thoughts on that description. It very much was a real village; albeit a portable one, but still a town-sized affair. There were over fifty huge tents, all of which were surrounded by men and a few women moving about preparing evening campfires. The smells of roasted fowl and lamb made her stomach tighten letting her know she was in fact very hungry after their trek to the desert. She saw men of every race and color, most wearing traditional Arab garb while several tall, regal looking black men wore brightly colored robes and carried long wooden shields and spears.

Gunarson's puzzled expression told her he'd never seen Nubians before.

"They are from the eastern coastlands," she told him. "They are mighty warriors who live in a jungle kingdom."

"Are we going to have to fight these ...Nubians??

Of course she had no answer for him and could only shrug her shoulders.

They were brought to the furthest end of the bivouac where a pen had been made of ropes tied around half a dozen palm trees. In it were both horses and camels. Next to this was another such enclosure, only this one was occupied by a dozen men in similar chains as those worn by the female samurai and her Viking ally.

The cart stopped and Bezi Akbar's men jumped from their horses and holding their curved swords at ready, motioned for Gunarson and Tishimi to get out. Awkwardly, having to make allowances for their manacled feet, the two prisoners managed to drop to their feet and were directed to join the others in the confines of the slave corral.

"Chain them to the strongest tree," Akbar directed his men. Having seen the two in action, he knew how dangerous they could be. Considering the Viking's near superhuman strength, he worried that once shackled to a palm tree, the northern barbarian might somehow manage to break his iron bracelets.

"At last, you have returned," a very familiar voice rang out from behind the sneaky Arab. He turned to see his master, Sheik Abu Sha marching towards him resplendent in white robes with blue piping stitched into the sleeves of his tunic that matched the loose indigo scarf hanging around his neck. His feet were encased in embroidered leather slippers. The young sheik was accompanied by two of his massive Tuareg bodyguards dressed in the dark blue garments of their clans; their heads and faces all but hidden by black scarves so that only their eyes were visible.

Bezi Akbar bowed at the waist as his master stood before him, then brought his fingertips to his chest, lips and forehead in a formal greeting. "Greetings and the peace of Allah the All-Wise, my master."

The handsome young leader merely nodded slightly, his handsome face hard and unyielding. "You took long enough, my friend. The contest begins tomorrow at first light."

"Forgive me, master, but finding warriors worthy of your attention and service was a formidable task and one I did not take lightly."

At this, Sheik Abu Sha looked beyond his agent at the two new prisoners now having their leg manacles connected with heavy chains wrapped around the base of a big oasis palm. "And you were successful in this task?"

"Yes, yes, master," Bezi's head bobbed up and down excitedly. "Please, come and see the two I have found. Each is a skilled warrior with unequalled fighting prowess."

The nervous agent led the sheik and his bodyguards to Ralph Gunarson and Tishimi Osara, both of whom were standing still eyeing their captors with cold, calculating glares as Akbar's men completed their work having carefully shackled them to the giant palm tree.

The sheik walked up to the Viking and examined him from the tip of his leather boots to the crown of his yellow-golden hair. He pulled on his trim goatee; a pleased expression in his eyes. "Indeed, this is a formidable beast of a man." He looked back at Bezi Akbar. "Maybe the equal of Molani even."

With that he turned his attention to the short, black-clad woman in chains next to the big northerner. A broad smile emerged on his face and he shook his head. "And what have we here? Some manner of jest, some ridiculous proposition to delight fools and simpletons?"

Versed in a dozen languages, Tishimi understood Abu Sha's words but offered absolutely no reaction to him. Her round, bronze face remained frozen and her rich green eyes continue to stare beyond him refusing to acknowledge his very presence.

Fearing his master's wrath, Bezi Akbar rushed to his side quickly. "I beg your indulgence, master. Do not dismiss this foreign female so rashly. She possesses a very special fighting technique unlike anything these I've ever witness before."

Intrigued, Abu Sha looked back at the woman. "Go on, Akbar."

"Master, in a crowded tavern brawl, I watched as she felled a dozen men, all more than twice her size and weight....with such apparent ease as if she were merely sweeping out a tent with a whisk broom."

The sheik's next words were sharp and threatening. "If you are lying to me, I will have your tongue ripped from your mouth."

Raising both hands up in front of himself, the agent took a step back and bowed. "Allah strike me dead, master, if every word I've uttered is not the truth in regards to this black haired demon woman."

"Very, well," Abu Sha decided on the spot. "Release her and let us see for ourselves if she is worthy to join my team of champions." Several of Akbar's mercenaries hurried to free Tishimi of her all her restraints, while everyone else in the area, from slaves to clansmen and camel herders stopped what they were doing and began to gather around.

Tishimi rubbed her wrist as they were chafed from the iron bracelets but made no other move.

Sheik Abu Sha turned to one of his Tuareg bodyguards and snapped his fingers. The man stepped up and faced Tishimi. "You will fight my man," the sheik commanded her."

Tishimi stood her ground. "No."

Abu Sha chuckled. "Very well, then you shall be beaten where you stand. Amir, strike her and continue to do so until I tell you to stop."

Without a second's hesitation, Amir the Tuareg swung his right arm at Tishimi. She pivoted on her back foot and the blow punched only air where her head had just been. He turned and tried a second time to hit her but the trained samurai danced away from him and once again his blow was ineffective. Now frustrated, the tall, heavy desert warrior gave

"If you are lying to me, Bezi…"

out a cry and launched himself at Tishimi. Without the slightest effort, she merely bent low and stepped around him so that he lost his balance with his arm swing and ended up in the dirt. Immediately those watching began to laugh, which only infuriated Amir all the more. He jumped to his feet and spun around looking for his target now standing several yards behind him, hands loosely at her side.

"Stop!" cried the sheik and all eyes turned to him. He looked at Tishimi and a wicked grin materialized on his tanned features. "Bezi Akbar!" he called out.

"Yes, my master."

"Take your knife and put it to the barbarian's throat. If the girl does not fight my man within the next few minutes, slit his throat."

Ralf Gunarson grunted as the agent rushed to him and produced a long, curved dagger from his tunic. While two other men pulled the Viking back against the thick palm stalk, Bezi Akbar reached up and put the edge of his blade against Gunarson's exposed throat.

"The choice is yours," Abu Sha told Tishimi. "You'd best decide quickly."

He looked at his Tuareg again. "Attack her...and show no mercy."

Amir propelled himself at Tishimi, his body leaning forward showing his intent to knock her off her feet with his superior build and strength.

For her part, Tishimi stood unmoving, her breath calm and shallow.

The distance between them evaporated and just as the Tuareg was almost atop her, Tishimi suddenly stepped off on her fight foot and her right hand shot out straight, the fist balled so that her knuckles struck first. They hit Amir in the middle of his chest with a loud smacking sound and his entire forward momentum came to a dead stop. A look of amazement and then pain fell over his eyes and then he toppled over backwards.

Tishimi had not moved an inch. Like liquid, she regained her fighting stance, only now her hands were held before her palms outward, as air blew out of her lungs.

Amir lay on the ground unconscious. She had felled him with a single blow.

Silence descended on the assembled crowd, many trying to grasp what they had just witnessed.

The sheik merely turned to his second Tuareg bodyguard named Wassim and said, "Your turn. Do not disappoint me."

Unlike his knocked out compatriot, Wassim, approached the lithe foreign she-devil cautiously, his hands out, his sandaled feet maintaining their balance. Amir had been a reckless idiot and paid the price. He was not about to make the same mistake. As he neared Tishimi, he watched her hands and feet for any sudden movement. When none came, he suddenly lunged forward but rather than use his fists, Wassim lashed out with a savage front kick.

Tishimi fell back, her hands crossed up before her. She blocked the Arab's kick and then immediately grabbed his ankle and spun him about. Off balance, Wassim fell to his side. The samurai skirted him carefully. From the ground, he tried kicking out at her again and she once again moved out of range. Angrily he climbed to his feet, shrugged the sand from his tunic and pants and then set about getting his revenge.

He came at Tishimi and attacked with a hard left punch. She moved inside the blow while spinning around so as to bring back her right elbow and smash it into his chest. Wassim's mouth gasped as air exploded out of his lungs and he dropped back…but not far enough. Tishimi then dropped her upper torso and at the same time drove her right leg back. The heel crushed the Taureg's groin and his eyes became twice their normal size. Doubling over to grasp his manhood, he never saw the second mule kick that caught him in the head and put out his lights.

He fell onto his side defeated and passed out.

The impromptu crowd suddenly erupted in loud cheers and applause. Regardless of Sheik's Abu Shaw's presence and obvious chagrin, they were unable to contain their enthusiasm for the brilliant display of martial skills they had just seen.

The sheik motioned to Bezi Akbar. "I've seen enough. You did better than expected, Akbar. There will be a reward in this for you."

"Thank you, master," the agent gushed, putting away his dagger. "I only live to serve you."

"Yes, I know." He looked over to see his other men once again chaining Tishimi alongside Gunarson. "See to it that they are well fed and treated. I want them both ready to fight when the games begin tomorrow morning."

"Your wish is ever my command, Sheik Abu."

At that, the satisfied leader approached his two newest fighters and calmly folded his hands behind his back as he addressed Tishimi. "That was a magnificent display, young lady. I am now confident that both you and your large companion here are quite capable of defeating any of the other fighters in the contest.

"Just remember this when you each of you is brought to the arena, the other will have a knife to his throat. If the one fighting loses the contest, my men will have the order to kill the other."

Gunarson looked down at Tishimi and then back at Abu Shaw. "Pray to your gods while you can, Arab, for when the time comes, I will kill you with my bare hands."

"Hahahaha, such bravado," Abu Shaw laughed. "I suggest you save it for tomorrow."

And with that he walked away, with Bezi Akbar following on his heels. Behind them others of his retinue splashed water on the two sleeping Tauregs in their attempts to revive them.

Tishimi watched the sheik disappear amongst the tents and looking up at Gunarson said, "Rest easy, Norseman. Our time will come."

The rest of the evening proved uneventful for Tishimi Osara and Ralf Gunarson. True to his word, Sheik Abu Sha made sure they were well fed and even had heavy horsehair blankets provided to sleep under once the desert air turned cold.

Eating their simple but nourishing meal, Tishimi had spoken with some of the other men held captive in the crude slave pen and learned, much like her and the Norseman, they too had been kidnapped by various sheiks or tribal leaders and were being forced to fight in the Contest of Champions. One of the men, a hunter from the western coast of Africa, shared what knowledge he'd gleaned during the course of his own captivity.

Thus did the lovely samurai learn of the powerful Sheik Turan Bey, the older brother of Abu Sha, and the originator of these so-called games. The prisoner painted the picture of a fat, self-indulgent monarch who loved nothing more than to watch others suffer under his heel. It was also known that he particularly enjoyed beating his younger sibling year after year because no one had ever been able to best Turan Bey's mighty black giant, Molani.

All these facts Tishimi took in and pondered as the stars began to appear in the blue-black firmament above. In the end, lying on her back beside her Viking companion while watching these bright points of silver light, the daughter of Master Swordsmith, Tokami Osara finally drifted into a deep, sound sleep.

The oasis camp was frantic as an agitated ant-hill the next morning as the desert chieftains and their entourages filed into the biggest tent staked out in the center of the site. Built in an octagon fashion, its eight canvas walls had been rolled up and secured to allow as many people access into the giant tent's interiors where the Contest of Champions was about to begin.

Ralf Gunarson and Tishimi, still in chains, were led into the tent along with the other slaves who were to participate in the contest. Shoving their way through the throng of excited desert tribesmen, the pair and their guards were taken to an area behind the seated sultans and shahs who sat at the head of a horseshoe-shaped vacant area. All of them were seated on piles of plush pillows and carpets surrounding the bare sandy floor in which the combat matches would take place. At the highest elevated seat was the plump Turan Bey, happily munching on a bowl of dates, while his brother, Abu Sha, sat slightly lower to his left.

Several musicians lost from sight behind the crowds were beating drums and playing flutes as most of the entire oasis populace filed into the great tent. Eventually all the chiefs were seated at the arena's edges with their tribesman standing behind them.

All the while Tishimi had been silently looking about her to judge the physicality of the other fighters, realizing she and Ralf would soon be facing many of them. The slave she had spoken with the previous evening had explained how the Contest of Champions was a simple elimination affair. Two men would fight; the loser was eliminated and the winner would go on to the next round to fight another opponent. This continued until all were defeated but one; the champion. He also added that no one had ever bested Turan Bey's mighty black slave, Molani.

Tishimi had done a quick head count and at her best estimation, there were at least forty men who would participate; most desert warriors and the handful of slaves she and Gunarson were a part of. Depending on how fast each bout lasted, she surmised the contest would last at least two to three days. More then enough time for she and the Viking to make good their escape.

Sheik Turan Bey shoved his empty bowl at one of his half naked harem girls and with a struggle, managed to get to his feet. He patted his big belly and then extruded his arms outward in greeting. "May the peace and blessings of Allah be with all of you, my brothers." To this the other chiefs bowed their heads and kissed their fingertips and touched their foreheads in proper response. "Once again I have the honor of welcoming you to our

Contest of Champions. I see many of you have new, untested warriors in your camps. Let's not keep them waiting any longer.

"LET THE GAMES BEGIN!"

With that the sheik took in the cheering applause of his colleagues and their people and dropped back into his cushioned seat. Swiftly, one of the sheik's primary scribes, an old fellow with a trim white beard, stepped into the middle of the open space and unfurled a huge paper scroll. He looked about the sea faces and then called out a name. A big Tuareg stepped out from where his tribe was standing and began to remove his tunic, scarf and turban. The scribe called out a second name and now a wiry slave who was being held to Tishimi's right was brought forth by his guards. Once in the fighting arena, his shackles were removed. Though smaller than the Tuareg, the freed prisoner was revealed to be agile and fit as his own tunic was removed. Like most desert folk, his skin was bronzed but there did not appear to be an ounce of fat on his body; it was all sinew and taut muscles.

Despite her distaste for the entire affair, Tishimi could not deny she was curious as to who would win this confrontation. After all, she was a samurai and her warrior's soul couldn't help but get caught up in such tests of martial abilities. She didn't have long to wait for as soon as the second man was ready, the scribe raced out of the sand and they went at each other.

The Taureg snarled and attempted to ensnare his opponent but the slave was quicker and danced around him at the same time punching him twice in the side and the small of the back. Infuriated, the tall man spun around and attacked again only to reap the same rewards; two hard fisted blows. Now the crowd was fully into the fight and shouting filled the tent. Many chiefs and their men were soon betting their dinars, gold and other coin on the outcome.

"He can't win," Gunarson said surprising Tishimi.

She looked up at him. "Who?"

"The small one."

"He seems to be holding his own," she replied. "As long as he..."

Just then, the wiry slave tripped while trying to evade the Tuareg. The Tuareg snagged him by the arm, pulled him backwards at the same time driving a hard right hand into his face. The slave fighter hit the ground senseless. The crowd yelled all the louder as the Tuareg held his hands up in victory, to the applause of his peers and the jeers of those who had bet against him.

Tishimi looked back at Gunarson and he grinned, "See."

She shrugged. The Tuareg was an untrained brute...as were most of these desert gladiators. She could have felled him in seconds. She began to wonder who she would have to fight when her turn came.

As the day progressed, each desert leader had an opportunity to put forth one of his fighters in the contest. Tishimi Osara continued to study each match carefully, gauging which of the winners she believed had some modicum of skill and might last beyond two rounds in the chain of contests.

By midday one of the three fights, she was personally concerned with was held. A rugged looking Berber with an ugly scar across the bridge of his nose entered the dueling area and then she heard Gunarson's name called out by the wizened scribe.

The blonde Viking chuckled. "At last. I was beginning to fall asleep, these so called fights are boring." And with that, he was escorted to the meet his opponent. The guards hastily undid and removed his shackles, while the Berber was stripping off his dark brown tunic.

Tishimi squeezed herself forward amongst two other slaves to look over the seated sheiks when she felt someone come up behind her and then a dagger blade slid up against her throat. It was the scum, Bezi Akbar, fulfilling his master's orders.

"Not a move," he cautioned her. She merely looked to the side to see Sheik Abu Sha looking back at her smugly, assuring himself she was now the incentive for the powerful Norseman to fight and win his fight.

The thing was, Tishimi knew, Ralf Gunarson had become genuinely interested in testing himself against these desert people. If there was something the Viking loved more than fighting, she had yet to discover what it could be. Now, once on the rough sand, he'd completely forgotten about her and was now giving his opponent all his attention.

Although Gunarson was bigger than the Berber, the latter was older and upon revealing his naked torso, his compact chest showed off half a dozen long scars that testified to the man's grim past.

But the young Viking wasn't really impressed at all and didn't even bother to remove his own leather jerkin. Instead, he swung his arms about loosely as he flexed his ham-sized biceps and waited for the fight to start. The second the scribe fled back into the safety of the audience, the Berber gave out a blood-curdling cry and charged the Northern seaman.

The cruel looking Berber punched Gunarson in the face hard.

Gunarson took a half step back, shook his head and then laughed. The Berber was stupefied and looked at his clenched fist as if it were a loyal dog that had failed him.

Meanwhile Gunarson continued to chuckle. Then, before anyone saw what happened, his right hand came up like a bolt of lighting and caught the scarred Berber under the jaw with a loud smacking noise that reverberated throughout the tent.

The Berber's eyes rolled up into their sockets so that only the whites were visible and then he fell over like a giant Norwegian oak, the impact of his body hitting the ground shook the packed sand.

It was the quickest fight of the day thus far. The audience erupted in a maddening cacophony of cheers and boos and lots of dinars changed hands.

The knife was removed from Tishimi's throat.

The second fight Tishimi had been anxious to see was that in which Sheik Bey's personal champion, Molani, made his first appearance in the small arena. It was mid afternoon and when his name was called, the black battler stepped into the tent, his raven black torso already naked and shiny with a thin layer of sweat. The crowd went wild with their approval as the blocky, heavy set slave strode to the centre spot and there raised both fists to his master in salute. Turan Bey nodded his head in approval and gave his brother a smug smile.

The luckless fellow to face the mighty Molani was a mercenary from the jungle wilderness of the Congo. Though tall and well constructed, he appeared like a dwarf next to the venerated champion.

"This should be good," Gunarson commented clearly impressed at the sight of Molani. Tishimi concurred realizing that unless they found a way to escape, the odds were very good her friend and the black giant would invariably have to face each other.

The contest lasted all of a minute as the mercenary did his best to avoid Molani's powerful hands but in the end the champion was too fast for him. He took hold of the challenger by his waist and easily lifted him off his feet all the while the mercenary was beating him savagely about the face and shoulders. Roaring in a primal rage, Molani raised the frightened warrior over his own head and then slammed him into the ground as if he were a piece of rotten food to be disposed of. The unlucky warrior landed head first and a loud crack was heard as his neck snapped like dry kindling and he died instantly.

At the sight of the cruel death, a somber silence descended on the assembly. Several of the dead fighter's companions came forth, picked him and hurriedly exited the tent.

Molani watched them go and then turned to the sheik and once again lifted up his arms. Once again the desert people screamed their approval of their hero.

Tishimi felt a shiver along her spine. Though several of the fighters had already been severely wounded and maimed, none had actually died. For the first time she understood that the predicament she and Gunarson were in was no laughing matter.

"This is not good," she said under her breath so only he could hear her words.

"No," the brave Viking agreed. "I may have to kill that one after all."

Of course, the third contest the female samurai awaited was her own which happened shortly before sunset. Once unchained, she made her way past those in front of her and when she appeared where all could see her several surprised gasps were heard. All betting ceased and then laughter began to bubble up amongst the gathering.

"Clearly, this is meant to be a joke?" Turan Bey questioned the fight scribe. Then he looked at the sea of faces. "Whose fighter does this...this... girl belong to?"

"She is mine," Abu Sha answered amused at the shocked look on his brother's round face. "And I assure you, she is a worthy advisory for any man here."

Turan Bay merely laughed, as did others. "Oh, dear brother, when will you ever grow up?"

"I'll bet you three hundred dinars she wins her contest," Abu Sha proclaimed.

"You have a bet," Turan Bey immediately shot back. "This will be the easiest prize I have ever won." He turned back to his old clerk. "Proceed with the fight."

At that, the white haired Arab called out a powerful looking Bedouin. He stepped onto the sand clad in desert attire and faced Tishimi. He slowly removed his scarf and turban to reveal an unshaven face of sharp angles with a hawk-like nose and beady brown eyes under curved brows. There was a cruel gleam in his eyes that said he would have no trouble fighting a woman.

The scribe backed out of the way and the two fighters approached each other. Tishimi saw the over confidence in the Bedouin's face and allowed herself to relax and remain calm. She would let her opponent bring about his own defeat which came speedily.

He lunged at her, his arms spread as to ensnare her. Tishimi planted her feet and the second he was within reach, punched him in the nose with her right fist. As his head rocked back, blood gushing from his nostrils, she took a step forward and drove her right elbow into his chest before grabbing his extended left arm. With this, she spun herself around, bent over and with a hard tug threw the helpless fellow over her back. He landed hard at her feet, where she promptly punched him in the forehead and ended the contest by knocking him unconscious.

For a second time, the entire male audience just stared at the defeated Bedouin and the black-clad female standing over him. Then they broke out in a hardy cheer.

"You can leave my three hundred dinars with one of my men," Abu Sha informed his red-faced brother. "This is getting to be a very enjoyable contest."

The remainder of the day was filled with more of the regular battles the audience had come to expect and by the time the last had finished, most of the chiefs were ready to retire to their own canvas pavilions.

Sinbad's sailors were returned to the slave section were they were given food and drink and then secured once again to the tall palm trees. Gunarson wasted little time in stretching out to his six foot, seven inch body and dropping off to sleep. His axe cutting snores soon were annoying many of the other slaves; all of them twisting away from the Viking in hopes of ignoring his awful nasal music.

...threw the helpless fellow over her back.

For her part, Tishimi sat with her back against the rough tree, her knees pulled up and simply reflected on what had transpired and wondered at what lay ahead come the next dawn. So caught up in her melancholy was she that she failed to notice the silent intruder until he was crouching up between her and the sleeping Viking.

Blinking, she was instantly alert, as the shadowy figure in Arab garb began to reach out a hand toward her. Like a striking cobra, Tishimi caught the wrist in her hands and twisted it back on itself.

"Sacre bleu!" Henri Delacrois cried out in a painful whisper. "Let go before you break my hand!"

"Henri!" She released his hand and he fell to his knees beside her, messaging his injured wrist. The scarf about his lower face fell away and in the moonlight, his handsome features smiled at her.

"Who else did you think would come after the two of you?" he answered while slapping the still sleeping Gunarson in the arm. "Sinbad would flay me alive if I were to tell him I'd lost two of his most able sailors."

"Huh…" Gunarson rolled over, still half clinging to sleep. "By Odin's beard…what?"

"Quiet, you blonde bear," Delacrois chided his friend. "Or you'll bring the guards down on us."

Now Gunarson's eyes were open wide and he sat up fully alert. "Henri! How did you find us?"

"Never mind that now," the archer said. "We have to get you two loose so we can flee this cursed desert and get back to the sea where we belong."

"That will not be easy," Tishimi stated and held up her shackled wrists. "Unless you know which of Abu Sha's men is holding the keys to our chains."

Delacrois looked from her to Gunarson and shook his head. "But we have to do something. I arrived here while those fights were in progress and was able to go unnoticed thus far. I've two horses tied on the other side of the camp. One is carrying your weapons."

"Which do us no good as long we are thus chained," Gunarson growled.

"So what do we do?" Delacrois' frustration was obvious. To have traveled all this way and now be stymied in his goal to set his companions free.

Tishimi looked up at the moon floating through the sky, her thoughts beginning to form a daring plan. One, that because of Delacrois' timely arrival might work. It was dangerous, but a bad plan was better than no plan at all.

"Listen to me, Henri," she looked into his eyes. "As we cannot escape now, then we will have to do it tomorrow…during the contest."

"What? That's insane. We'll be surrounded by hundreds of these Arab dogs. What chance do the three of us have of defeating them?"

"We need not defeat them all," the lovely samurai continued. "Only one of them."

With their plans set, Sinbad's lieutenants were ready to play their individual parts when the sun rose the following day and the Contest of Champions resumed in the big tent of Sheik Turan Bey. Once again Delacrois was able to walk in amongst the desert folks, keeping his face scarf above his nose and carrying a heavy sack over his shoulder. In this were weapons belonging to his two shipmates.

Much as Tishimi had expected, the second round quickly halved the number of the participants. Both she and Gunarson won their second fights easily as did Molani the African bruiser. Then by midday, there only remained four combatants and the crowd was so charged up one could feel the electricity in the open air pavilion.

Gunarson's prediction had come to past. He was set to battle Molani. But first Tishimi had to fight another big African named Chaka; a towering figure who only wore a tiger-skinned loin cloth and had complex tattoos painted all over his brown torso. His arms and legs were overly long and sinewy and he reminded Tishimi of a human grasshopper.

Unlike her previous two opponents, the Japanese maiden instinctively saw in her opponent a cunning foe worthy of respect and caution. Once the fight had begun, Chaka approached her slowly, his long body in a crouch, wary as in what manner she would strike. It was obvious he had studied her own bouts and was purposely staying out of range of her flying fists and kicks. Whereas Tishimi had seen the jungle bred warrior outsmart his first two opponents and ultimately felled each with graceful kicks to the head. So, as much as she watched his face as the two move about each other, she was also aware of his bare feet as they slid across the sand.

Suddenly Chaka pivoted and his right leg started to come up. Tishimi turned to it bringing her arms up in a defensive X only to realize too late she'd been tricked. Instead of throwing his right leg, Chaka had swiftly planted it on the ground continuing his spin so that it was his left leg that suddenly came up and around and hit Tishimi. It caught her in the chest and sent her flying backwards into the air.

Getting control of her body in midair, the trained samurai allowed her trajectory to flip her completely thus landing back on her heels in an upright stance, both hands out and ready for any follow-up attack. At the sight of her amazing recovery, Chaka grinned and nodded his head slightly in a sign of respect. Tishimi repeated the gesture then launched her own attack.

Giving out with a piercing, "KIA!!" she ran at the tall fighter with all the speed she could muster. Startled, he started to move out of her path. But Tishimi had anticipated this reaction and suddenly jumped forward off the ground, her entire body shooting upward like a striking black eagle feet first. As the arc of her leap reached the now confused Chaka, Tishimi twisted her body and her right foot kicked the side of Chaka's head with the punch of a mule. The lanky African sprawled on the sand and stayed there unmoving.

Tishimi landed beyond him in her fighting stance and when she saw he was defeated, she relaxed, stood erect and dropped her hands to her side.

She looked around at the crowd and spotted Delacrois hiding in the back watching her; his merry eyes acknowledging her victory.

Abu Sha's guards led her out of the arena and back to where Gunarson stood behind the two brother sheiks. As they proceeded to undo his chains, she looked up at her friend and grinned. "Your turn."

And so began the one contest all had been anticipating between the venerated champion, Molani, and the blonde Viking. Gunarson had soundly defeated his previous opponents effortlessly as if he was swatting away flies and won the favor of the crowd in so doing. But now the desert people were equally divided as they began to wager amongst themselves as to the outcome of what would surely be a monumental battle of two near superhuman warriors.

As before, Molani entered from outside and ignoring Gunarson altogether, once more saluted his liege, Sheik Turan Bay.

The older chieftain sneered at his sibling. "Now, my dear Abu, we will once again put an end to your foolish dreams of victory."

Abu Sha had all he could do to keep silent, knowing any retort at this point would be pointless. He looked at the fight coordinator and waved his hands at him impatiently.

"What are you waiting for? Let the contest begin."

And with that, the scribe rushed out of the open space and Molani slowly turned to face Ralf Gunarson. Both men calmly stood like living statues, each eyeing the other with a cold, calculating glare; each preparing themselves for the ultimate challenge to their strength and endurance.

Then, as if they were joined mentally, both marched to the middle of the arena and slammed into the other. Their arms were out first and as their bodies collided, each grabbed the others hands so their fingers intertwined, black with white. The Viking was mere inches taller than Molani and his ice-like blue eyes bore into the African's brown orbs. Molani had a flat nose and now it flared as he used all the power in his body to bear down on the Norsemen. Each man dug his feet into the hard earth and continued to strain against the other, their hands still locked together above their heads.

Sweat began to bead on their brows and each man's breath came in ragged gaps mingled with primal growls, each unwilling to yield. The crowd had quieted when it realized that this would be no contest of mindless fists plummeting wildly but instead it was to be a battle of raw strength as each man stood his ground refusing to give an inch to the other.

From deep in his body Molani gave out an animal like cry and his arms seemed to swell as they slowly and methodically began to drive the Viking's body down. Seeing this slight change, wages continued to be bet and Molani's fans urged him on all the louder.

Meanwhile Tishimi watched the contest stoically knowing fully well that if Gunarson lost, they're desperate plan would be impossible. Everything hinged on his winning. She closed her eyes and prayed to her honored ancestors.

Seeing the tide turning, Molani, a once former prince, continued to apply pressure on the younger Viking. Inch by slow inch he was driving Gurnarson to his knees. The blonde haired sailor went down on one knee and the audience gasped, half seeing new dinars coming their way, the other half dreading their parting.

But the Viking wouldn't give up and no matter how much Molani bore down on him, Gunarson held him off, his body locked in its kneeling position. Somewhere in his soul he could hear the songs of his people as they went into battle. He could see them in his mind's eye wielding their battle-axes and broadswords while they sailed across the open seas conquering all who dared block their destiny.

It was a beserker's rage that began to fill the lad's veins and with a guttural cry, he looked up at the maddened eyes of his foe and he laughed. He began to renew his upward force until he rose up off his knee like a behemoth rising from the depths of the ocean. Molani's expression was that of sheer surprise. In his entire life no man had ever withstood his might and yet this brash, white skinned Norseman was doing just that. Desperately the African tried to summon more strength only to discover it was long since depleted.

Once again both men were facing each other squarely, the Viking's stare now intractable as he glared at Molani. Then without warning Gunarson smashed his forehead into the African's face. The blow dazed Molani and he stepped back, his first ever retreat in combat. Gunarson didn't wait but repeated the blow again smashing his own hard head into the opponent's face. Blood spurted from Molani's nose as his eyes lost their focus.

He staggered backwards and Gunarson let go of his hands. With a mighty roar he clutched his hands together and using them like a hammer, struck the now defenseless Molani across the face.

Unable to stand, the black giant fell to knees and then toppled over onto his side.

Everyone watching had been holding their breaths seeing Turan Bay's champion fall still not believing their eyes. Then, when Molani failed to rise, pandemonium reigned as the desert Arabs exploded in a deafening applause.

Finally Molani stirred and rolled over onto his back. He brought up his right hand to wipe the blood off his face and looked up at the man who had defeated him.

"You are the champion now," Molani said in a deep, rich timbered voice. "NOOOOO!!!"

Everyone's heads turned to the raised seats to see Turan Bay jumping to his feet, his beefy face ripe with anger. "NO! NO! NO!"

The fat sheik started down of his couch of stuffed pillows, waving his arms all about. As he went past another chieftain, he reached over and snatched a small, four foot hand whip made of horsehair that camel drovers used to spur their beasts.

"Fail me, you ignorant, stupid savage!" he bellowed holding up the quirt as he moved past Gunarson who, like everyone else, was bemused by the sheik's flamboyant outrage.

Then, standing over his slave, Turan Bay brought down the whip and began to flay him with it. "Stupid, dumb animal! You cost me a fortune! After all I've done for you! I should have you put to death immediately!"

With each curse, the sheik struck at the confused Molani who held up his arms to protect his face which wore an expression of shame and bewilderment.

"Forgive me, master," he begged. "I did my best."

"Well, your best wasn't good enough," Turan Bay kept whipping the fallen fighter. "I will see you punished, you dumb, ignorant black ape."

Then, just as Turan Bay was about to swing his arm down again, a powerful hand reached over his shoulder and tore the whip from his hand almost causing him to stumble and fall.

He whirled around to see Ralf Gunarson holding the quirt in his hands and leaning down over him.

"Enough, you prancing fat fool! You have no right to treat this man as if he were an animal. He is a proud and noble warrior and you aren't fit to lick his sandals!"

It was one of the longest speeches Tishimi Osara had ever heard her friend utter. Even from her position, she could see the menace in his crystal blue eyes. This was not part of their plan but she knew it offered all of them another opportunity; if they were able to take advantage of it. Even shackled, she began to push her way through the crowd and Abu Sha whose entire attention was on the scene playing out in the arena.

"Why you barbaric cretin," Tuan Bay spat. "How dare you defy me!" He looked to his tribesman and pointed up at Gunarson. "What are you waiting for? Draw your blades and kill this man! I command it!"

Two of the closest Berbers pushed out of the crowd and drew their scimitars but before they could take another step, there was a twanging sound and both were struck with arrows; dead center in their chests. As they collapsed, all eyes searched for whoever it was that had so skillfully fired those arrows.

"There!" a desert dweller yelled and pointed to Henri Delacrois, standing with his longbow in his hands having just notched another arrow in it. Those around him parted as best they could not wanting to be his next target.

"GET HIM!" Turin Bay shouted. He was so furious, spittle sprayed form his mouth.

But before anyone could react to his command, Molani suddenly rose up behind his master and grabbed him by the shoulder. He spun the screaming sheik around to face him and then wrapped his huge hands around Bay's thick neck. With a heave, he lifted him off the sand and using what strength he had left, hoisted him high as his fingers began to squeeze the life out of the cruel Bedouin sheik.

Upon seeing this, Abu Sha started to get up only to suddenly have Tishimi appear directly behind him. With a swift toss, she had thrown the chain connecting her wrist manacles about his neck and jerked him back into his pillows. Pulling it back tightly, she leaned her head next to his and whispered, "Move and you will share your brother's fate."

One of Abu Sha's men saw Tishimi's assault and whipped out his scimitar and started to swing it at the back of her head. At the same moment another of Delacrois arrows flew straight hitting the man in the throat. He gurgled, blood spilling from his lips as he fell over. Tishimi pulled the chain tighter causing Abu Sha's eyes to double and the air was cut from his lungs.

Not wasting any time to see if his arrow had hit true, the dashing Gaul raced over to the arena and threw the heavy sack he'd been carrying into Gunarson's arm. The Viking dropped it at his feet and peeling it open smiled from ear to ear. From it he procured his twenty pound battle axe and began hefting high for all to see.

"They're killing the sheik," one brave soul had the courage to cry out what was obvious to all. At that Gunarson charged at the crowd whipping his double-edged weapon and the crowd parted exposing the foolish man who had spoken. He looked up in time to see Gunarson's blade come down and with a single swipe sliced his head from his body.

"Anyone else eager to visit Valhalla?" Gunarson asked, blood smearing his tunis. "Tis a fine day to die."

Meanwhile Sheik Turan Bay's feet had stopped their kicking as his foul spirit departed and he died as he had lived, cruelly. Seeing he was holding a lifeless corpse, Molani turned and tossed the sheik's body into the front gathering of chiefs. It landed atop several of them not quick enough to get away.

Now Molani came stand back to back with his new allies, Gunarson brandishing his gory axe and Delacrois ready with another razor sharp barb to let fly. The tableau was frozen as the crowd of vengeful desert folks remained rooted to the ground, no one foolhardy enough to challenge this deadly trio.

Seeing the stalemate, Tishimi wisely loosened the iron chains pressing in on Abu Sha's windpipe. He gulped air like a fish cast from its brook.

Once more, the deadly samurai spoke to him softly. "What happens next is up to you, Abu Sha. Demand vengeance and my friends and I will deliver you a bloodbath unlike anything you have ever seen." She tugged on the chain to emphasize her point. "And you will be the first to die."

"Enough," he managed to croak. "Let me loose…and I'll let you live."

"And release all your slaves…including Molani…without further retribution."

"Yes, yes. Damn woman, I swear on Allah's beard."

Tishimi had no reason to trust Abu Sha save her knowledge of human nature and she was betting on his own innate greed to prove their salvation. She lifted the chains up over his neck thus freeing him.

Massaging his bruised throat, the younger sheik stood up and addressed his people. "There will be no more fighting. All of you sheath your blades and listen to me." He pointed to the body of his dead brother. "My brother was a heartless man who brought about his own doom. He ignored the teachings of Allah and the ways of peace."

"But he was your brother," one of the chieftains interrupted.

"Yes, and now that he is dead, I am then new Sheik…am I not?"

The man refused to meet Sha's look and bowed his head. "Yes, my sheik. You are our new leader."

"Then, I order these people released at once." He looked back at Tashimi and remembered his promise. "As well as all the other captives. Let them go immediately. This ugly affair is finished. There will be no more such gatherings amongst our people.

"Now somebody get these bodies out of here before they stink up my tent."

Hours later, and miles away, four riders on horseback traversed the wasteland making their way north to the sea. Sinbad's three lieutenants, all cleaned up and fed, role along with the freed Molani. Hoping to find someway to return to his African home along the eastern coast, Delacrois had suggested he return with them to port and there perhaps they could convince their Captain Sinbad to bring him home aboard the *Blue Nymph*. Having never been aboard a sailing ship, the once former jungle prince was anxious to experience this new adventure with his new found companions.

As they crested a long twisting dune, Gunarson looked back at the awkwardly wrapped figure stretched over the fifth horse which they had brought along as a pack animal. "I think we've gone far enough," he said.

The others stopped their horses and watched as he slid off his and walked to the trailing horse. He grabbed the package and pulled it off the horse's back to let it fall onto the hot sand. "OOFF!" sounded from the package.

Gunarson kneeled and ripped over the tightly wrapped cloth to expose a frightened Bezi Akbar, who immediately shielded his eyes from the harsh glare of the sun.

"Infidel dogs, why have you done this to me? It was Abu Sha who ordered your capture. I was merely his servant!"

"Which is why we decided not to kill you, Bezi." Gunarson pulled him to his feet. "Now, take off your pants and slippers."

"What?"

"You heard him," Delacrois added. "Remove the items....or would you prefer my blond friend gut you here for the buzzards to feed upon?'

The once cocky Arab looked at the three riders and realized he would find no further mercy from them. He tore off his slippers and began tugging down his baggy pants.

"I'll die out here," he began to whine.

Tishimi looked up at the sky and shook her head. "We've only been traveling several hours." She pointed back the way they had come. "You should make it back to the oasis before sunset. Slightly sunburned, but still alive. Thank your ancestors that is all we do to you."

Bezi Akbar saw their would be no changing their minds and finally resigned himself to his fate. He started walking back amongst the tracks their horses had made, his tender feet hopping on the burning sand, his spindly legs wobbling.

"Ouch! Ouch!"

Soon he was lost from sight and Gurnarson remounted his horse.

As the four once again turned northward, Henri Delacrois rode up beside the blonde Viking and scratched his goatee. "I am still wondering, my friends," he began, "what would have happened if the two of you would have actually had to fight each other."

Gunarson was surprised by the statement and looked from Delacrois to Tishimi. "Surely you jest, Henri."

"Non, mon ami." Delacrois held up his hands. "Alas, now we will never know."

"What?" Gunarson was irate. "There is no way Tishimi could ever beat me. Tell, him, Tishimi."

Tishimi Osara gave Gunarson a whimsical half-smile and said, "Maybe. And then, maybe not."

"Huh!" Gunarson's temper began to flare. "You are both crazy! There's no way I could ever lose to a girl...NO WAY!!!"

Tishimi and Delacrois started laughing as they spurred their horses to a faster gallop. They were eager to leave the desert behind and get back to the sea where they belonged. Their laughter echoed over the landscape.

The End

The Warriors Three

When I first cooked up the idea of doing a new series of Sinbad stories, part of the fun was shaking things up a wee bit. Ergo, we wanted a black Sinbad, one with a royal background. Then I thought it was great to crew his ship with an international cast and thus created Henri Delacrois, the Gauish archer, Ralf Gunarson, the blonde Viking and my persona favorite, Tishimi Osara, the small, deadly female samurai. Once I'd written the bible for the series and passed it around to our staple of Airship 27 writers, I quickly learned that lots of other writers loved these characters and were really eager to work with them. And so three anthologies and a full length novel later, here we are with yet another collection of tales. As I read the stories being turned in, the itch to personally get into this world became overwhelming.

So what if Sinbad went off on some kind of secret mission with the Caliph and in his absence he gave his crew shore-leave? Knowing these three, I began imagining it wouldn't take them long to get into some kind of outlandish, dangerous adventure. The temptation became a story idea thus "The Desert Contest" came about and my first chance to write the characters I'd created. I had a blast and I hope you did as well. Thanks for supporting the series.

RON FORTIER – Comics and pulps writer/editor best known for his work on the Green Hornet comic series and Terminator – Burning Earth with Alex Ross. He won the Pulp Factory Award for Best Pulp Short Story of 2011 for "Vengeance Is Mine," which appeared in Moonstone's The Avenger – Justice Inc. and in 2012 for "The Ghoul," from the anthology Monster Aces. He is the Managing Editor of Airship 27 Productions, a New Pulp Fiction publisher and writes the continuing adventures of both his own character, Brother Bones – the Undead Avenger and the classic pulp hero, Captain Hazzard – Champion of Justice.

You can find him at (www.Airship27.com)

SINBAD and the SINISTER STATUE

by Lee Houston Jr.

"**I** do not like this!" Captain Sinbad El Ari swore as he stared at the scene before him. Other than their final destination at its center, there were no other structures on the island. The clearing at the end of the open trail was lush, green, and well maintained. An oddly pristine setting for such a valued treasure, compared to some of the other places that housed riches. "After all we have been through to reach this point, I find it too quiet."

"I agree Captain," said Ralf Gunarson, a long-haired, blonde Viking from the far-off North, sailing with Sinbad in search of grand adventures and great battles. "After the storms, the whirlpool that suddenly appeared in otherwise calm waters, and the sea monsters, it seems odd to find an open path before us now. One would expect another mammoth monstrosity, or at least an army of men to challenge us at this point," he added unhappily. The big man reveled in overwhelming confrontations.

"Has anyone else noticed that we have neither seen nor heard any wild creatures since setting foot upon this island? Not even a single birdsong; nor has anything taken wing as we approached," Sinbad continued with concern in his voice. "This island is lifeless."

The rest of his companions, the shore party from their ship the Blue Nymph, nodded and muttered in agreement. "It is unnatural!" someone else agreed, and many made a warding gesture against evil.

"Begging your pardon Captain, but that is not entirely true," said Govad the sailor, appointed by First Mate Omar as temporary leader of the men

87

assisting Sinbad. "There are plenty of these strange plants about," he added, pointing to the walls of vines that bordered the trail.

While their path was devoid of them, the surrounding jungle was completely filled with gnarled, dark brown, flowerless creepers with sharp thorns that twisted in and around themselves so much that they formed a natural barrier. Not so much as a stray green leaf could be seen upon the almost impenetrable plant wall, for it towered over even Gunarson, who was the tallest member of the shore party.

"There are no insects either. *Not* that I am complaining about their absence," commented Henri Delacrois, perfectly willing to admit how much he hated the tiny creatures. "Yet this oppressive heat is just as bothersome," he added, once more wiping the sweat from his brow with a fancy handkerchief. The man from Gaul, an expert archer beyond compare, sailed with Sinbad in hopes of making his fortunes in foreign lands to one day return home wealthy enough to put the ill-advised dalliances of his past behind him.

"If we are all agreed that a trap may lie ahead, then of what nature is it?" asked Tishimi Osara, as she kept her emerald green eyes trained on their surroundings, ready to defend her friends and crewmates at the first hint of danger. From the mysterious East, her native clothing of black silk leggings and tunic were hot and clung to her lithe body, but she uttered no complaints, for her outfit granted the greatest freedom of movement. Although not as accustomed to the heat as some of her companions were, the female samurai would endure whatever she had to in order to support her captain.

"That I do not know," admitted Sinbad, showing no sign of discomfort, "but at least the Emir of Opres' directions were correct. Ahead lies our final destination."

With that declaration, everyone looked up at the massive structure looming before them. Bigger than any palace ever seen before, the round building was capped by an enormous golden dome, whose top was lost somewhere in the clouds. Its true height remained unknown, for no one could gaze directly at the dome because of the way it brightly reflected the sunlight.

"Impressive. Yet how does the area around it remain open?" asked Henri, noting the flat, bare ground that stretched out several feet from them and the inner boundary of the jungle before touching the bottom of the steps that led up to the raised base of the structure.

"It's sorcery," Ralf rumbled, gripping the handle of his double-bladed battleaxe firmly.

Tishimi disagreed. "More likely proof that attendants must live nearby, or that the enemy awaits within, ready to attack us when we are out in the open unprotected."

"Possibly," Sinbad admitted. "All the Emir could say about this area was that his revered ancestors hid their most prized possession in this remote spot generations ago, to keep their enemies from obtaining it. The only other information he had was written on the old map he gave me. Even if they did scout the surrounding area back then, much would have changed in the passing years."

"Why did he not send one of his own ships on this voyage?" Henri asked uneasily.

"We are here because the previous Emir of Opres was a man I knew well, and was proud to call a friend. That was why I agreed to this voyage, although our payment upon returning will be quite grand," replied Sinbad. "His successor, a nephew, hired us to retrieve the Statue of Kumana, believing now is the time for its rightful return to honor his uncle's memory. He desires its arrival to be a surprise."

"Then none of his people would be here now caring for this place," realized Ralf.

"True, but that does not mean no one else could have discovered and claimed it for themselves in the time since," Tishimi pointed out.

Except for its dome and the building's rather plain looking stone foundation, the rotunda seemed to be composed entirely of finely polished white marble. A multitude of thick columns were evenly spaced to support the huge roof, with just enough of a gap between each one to let a person pass. A single set of gradually narrowing stairs led up to the top of the edifice's raised base, which was taller than an average man's height above the cleared jungle floor. The bottom step could easily accommodate five people abreast, but the top one was just wide enough to allow only one person at a time through a specific group of columns. It was a curious layout, likely designed to keep large groups from attacking all at once.

The shore party approached cautiously, prepared to fight or retreat as needed, but no attack from any direction was forthcoming. Once at the top step, with Ralf and Tishimi just below him, Sinbad observed that there were actually a multitude of entrances available. There was just enough space between the outer edge of the dome's support columns and the foundation's border for people to walk around the rotunda single file. Sinbad felt a steady, humid breeze, indicating the structure was open all around. This meant, if desired, one could enter at any point—although the sea captain could not fathom the reasoning behind such an arrangement.

"Why build this place?" wondered Henri. "Would it not have been simpler to bury the statue, or hide it in a cave?"

"Perhaps," agreed Sinbad. "There is a warning of possible traps on the map, but the new Emir could not say what they might be."

"Could not, or would not?" asked Ralf. "You have many enemies Captain."

"One cannot live a full life without making a few, but I am not so easily outmaneuvered," said Sinbad confidently.

His friends positioned themselves on the lower steps, ready to act if necessary. The remaining crew stayed on the ground at the staircase base, alert and awaiting the Captain's next order as he thrust his scimitar, a Persian curved sword, within the space between the two columns in front of him.

Striking only air, he repeated the procedure on the outer side of each. "No traps here," he said confidently, as Sinbad stepped forward between the columns long enough to peer inside.

"It is as black as a moonless night within," he called back to the others. "There is no light from any source, and it looks as if the interior is made of a dull, dark material that swallows all light," he added, pointing to what little could be seen of the sun shining on the floor between support columns. "Someone will have to go inside with a torch and scout the area."

"Let me, Captain," volunteered Abdul, a young sailor eager for plunder.

As Sinbad nodded his acceptance, Abdul motioned impatiently to Govad, who carried two burlap sacks. One held an old sail to be used for securing their prize, while the other contained prepared torches. Selecting one, the volunteer approached a fellow sailor who carried a small wooden cask of oil. Abdul soaked the cloth covered end of the torch in the black substance before its bearer resealed his cask. Then, at a safe distance away, Abdul lit it with a fire striker set of flint and pyrite.

As Tishimi and Ralf repositioned themselves to allow Abdul access, he came up the staircase to stand next to his Captain and bowed briefly. Sinbad spoke quietly, advising caution before the brave man entered, with sword arm bearing his weapon and torch in the other hand, lighting his way.

Abdul's form, torch and all, was soon swallowed by the darkness. Only his voice echoed through the impenetrable gloom within.

"This place is as vast inside as it appears outside Captain. I can barely see anything past the edge of the torchlight," shouted Abdul a moment later, his words sounding quite distant one moment, close by the next; making his progress almost impossible to trace.

"What *can* you see?" asked Sinbad, yelling in return; but there was no reply. An eerie silence reigned for long, tense moments before a blood curdling scream announced the final terror of a dying man.

"Henri, I want a flaming arrow shot in there!" Sinbad ordered.

"Oui, Mon Capitane," replied Delacrois, as he turned to Wasif, the sailor assigned to assist him on this expedition. Black of hair and dark of skin, the man withdrew an arrow from the quiver he wore, but these were different than the shafts in the pouch on Delacrois' back, for each had a small rag tied behind the arrow head.

Wasif dipped the arrow into the same cask Abdul used, and then handed it to Henri. The archer nocked it as Tishimi and Ralf cleared the way to allow him to join Sinbad at the rotunda entrance.

"And my target is...?" inquired Henri, peering into the darkness between columns.

"Abdul safely walked for forty paces, by my count, before something happened. Aim for the floor about forty-five paces inward," requested Sinbad, who was now standing to the right of what he considered the entrance.

Henri backed down one step, to be more even with the floor inside, as Sinbad ignited the flammable material on the arrow. "It will not last long, but this little star will shine as brightly as the sun overhead," said the archer, sighting before pulling the bowstring taut.

Releasing the arrow, the flaming shaft sailed through the darkness, flying above the floor at about the height of a man's waist. As it traveled, Henri watched, confident of his ability to judge the distance, even within such a dark place.

He was surprised when the fiery projectile disappeared from sight!

"It is as if the floor does not exist," declared Delacrois.

"True," agreed Sinbad. "There must be a pit hidden within the darkness, but until we explore further, we will not know how big it actually is."

"I am prepared to face whatever lies ahead," said Henri, nocking a traditional arrow into the bow from the quiver on his back. "With proper lighting, of course!"

"As am I," said Sinbad thoughtfully, "but we must also be more cautious. The darkness within likely hides more than one danger."

"What do you propose, Mon Capitaine?"

"Scouting the perimeter first. Tishimi, you and Ralf stay along the base of the rotunda, walking in opposite directions from here. Govad, you and I will do the same along the upper rim," ordered Sinbad. "The rest of you, stay alert and be ready to enter this place upon our return. No one else goes in until then."

"Anything to report?" asked Sinbad, when the quartet met at the halfway point.

"The base of this place appears solid, with no sign of any hidden entrances, and there are no breaks within the jungle wall other than the one through which we entered," said Ralf. "No tracks either, other than our own."

"So we are truly alone?"

"If there is an enemy present, they are very clever at concealing their presence," Tishimi answered.

"I can see the ocean," replied Sinbad, from his higher position on the outer ring. "The vines do not grow along the edge of the cliffs. Yet from here, I cannot say how close the Blue Nymph could come to the island, let alone whether or not the rocks are surmountable."

"We will look it over before resuming our journey," promised Tishimi. "We may need an alternate escape route."

Sinbad agreed, then asked, "What about escape routes from this building?"

Ralf shook his head. "I only saw the one staircase," he said, a fact to which the others concurred. "We'd have to jump down, and then run or fight."

"I assume you never looked upward. There is a large opening above our heads," Tishimi informed them.

Everyone craned their heads skyward and saw a roughly circular hole, the bottom of which lay along the base of the golden dome.

"What can that be for?" wondered Govad.

"Not ventilation," answered Sinbad. "There are plenty of opportunities for air to enter the rotunda between columns."

"It is crudely made," commented Ralf, noting the rough edges, "as if someone added it later."

"Yet another question that needs answering," observed Tishimi.

"It is time to move on. We shall finish our journeys back to the others, and then enter this place to find the statue," said Sinbad.

Back on board the Blue Nymph, the rest of the crew were going about their respective duties under the watchful eye of Omar. The First Mate and Master of the Crew had stayed in the Captain's absence, fretting about both the safety of the ship and his closest friend.

When they thought he was not listening, Omar could hear the sailors talk amongst themselves. Some grumbled about whatever unknown dangers might be faced this time. Others told stories about past voyages or wenching. A few even prayed, but as long as their tasks were performed, he said nothing.

Only those idle incurred Omar's wrath. The men off duty who wished to rest or gamble amongst themselves could only do so below deck. Yet the First Mate knew that there were no finer sailors or fighters in all the world. Sinbad only hired the best, and at a moment's notice, they would be on their feet at battle stations; hoisting anchor, raising sails, or manning the oars.

All appeared calm, but what no one had yet to notice was that the jungle foliage was slowly creeping closer to the shoreline. No one that is but Haroun, the cabin boy.

Yet he did not dare say anything and bring Omar's wrath down upon himself. After all, even if he was right in seeing them move closer to the water, it was just plants. What harm was there in them?

As the quartet reunited with the rest of their party back by the lone staircase, Tishimi announced, "The cliff face itself will be easy to surmount. The problem is the shoreline. The waters are rocky, with only one possibly clear channel for a small boat to pass. Yet if the tide is against it when the attempt is made…"

"Let that be my concern," said Sinbad, understanding best the ways of the sea. "For now, we will proceed cautiously and see what kind of reception awaits us."

Henri handed him a torch, whose cloth end had been well soaked in oil while he was away. Lighting it off the flame of another, the captain led the way with his scimitar drawn. Entering single file, he was followed by Tishimi. With her katana in one hand and short sword in the other, she was unable to hold a torch and depended upon the rest of the shore party to provide light. However, her black outfit blended in well with the surrounding environment, always a benefit in battle.

Behind her were two sailors bearing supplies. Piruz and Sohrab each had a coil of rope slung over their shoulders and wrapped around their chests, freeing their hands to hold swords and torches.

Henri and Wasif were in the middle of the procession. The archer had his bow partially drawn to shoot at a moment's notice, while his temporary assistant held a torch overhead to provide them both light. Merikh was behind them with only his sword drawn, because he now carried the sailcloth. Ziyad walked after him, lighting the way as Bedr followed, needing both hands to bear the small cask of oil. Govad trailed them with the next to last lit torch, the rest within his sack. Ralf brought up the rear, torch in one hand and his battleaxe held ready in the other, his sword in a hilt strapped on his back. The Viking was very proficient with either weapon, but preferred the axe in close quarters.

The rotunda was roomy inside, with nothing but wide open space visible as far as the torch light carried. There was no place for an enemy to hide, so Sinbad had reconfigured his crew into a row to spread their light farther, though he remained in front.

Counting paces, he called a halt to the procession short of the last safe step. "This is where we lost Abdul," Sinbad told them unhappily, as he stared down at the first obstacle in their path. "It is a pit, but wider than I thought it would be, and appears to encompass the entire interior like a moat, making it totally unavoidable regardless of one's entry point."

The curved trench stretched outward as far as the eye could see. There was no immediate sign of the bottom, with dark walls of the same ebony material as the rest of the interior. It was far too wide to jump across, and the smooth interior angled so that a helpless victim would find no purchase before falling to his death.

"At first, I thought its concealment in the darkness was what made this pit trap effective. Now, I am uncertain how we shall cross it," admitted Sinbad. "Even if I had the foresight to bring it with us, the opening is wider than the Blue Nymph's gangplank."

"Then how did those who built this place travel onward?" asked Henri, from his position in line.

"An excellent question. Let us see if there is a way, but stay within sight of each other in case more surprises await us," warned Sinbad.

As they spread out to search the interior, Govad bent down near the edge of the pit to examine it more closely. Shining his torch over the opening, he said, "It's at least the length of the ship's hull to the bottom, but all I can see are piles of skeletons, with poor Abdul's lifeless body atop them."

"Bare bones?" asked Ralf.

"Mostly," confirmed Govad.

"A disappointing end," commented the Viking grimly. "A man should die fighting!"

"Abdul was brave to volunteer to walk into the unknown," Sinbad said, to keep the other men from protesting Ralf's blunt assessment.

"What picked their bones clean, time or predators?" wondered Tishimi aloud, walking with the rope bearers.

"That matters not. This pit has claimed its last victim today," declared Henri, standing a few feet away from the others. "We have found something," he added, pointing to where Wasif was shining his torch.

Walking over to the archer, Sinbad saw five small squares faintly etched within the otherwise solid ebony of the floor. Grouped together, depending upon what angle you viewed them from, they reminded him either of the basic shape of a diamond or an 'X'.

"By design, it was hard to find," admitted the archer. "Except for these thin lines, this floor is quite smooth. What do you think it might be?"

"Hopefully, it is the key. Let us see what it opens," said the captain.

As the toe of his boot pressed upon the center square, Sinbad's weight caused it to sink a little lower into the floor. A strange noise, like scraping and creaking, could be heard. Nothing living made that sound.

"Look, there was some kind of bridge hidden within the floor!" announced Merikh, who was searching along the pit's edge. "It crossed the opening and went into a hole on the other side to keep it in place, but not at the same spot we were. Abdul's remains are to the left of it."

Setting aside the question of what the other four squares might do, Ziyad was already volunteering to scout ahead before Sinbad could ask.

"I will go forth as bravely as Abdul did," the sailor declared, but Sinbad ordered a rope tied around his waist first. If the wooden ramp could not bear Ziyad's weight, there would still be a chance of rescuing him.

However, the precaution was unnecessary, for Ziyad crossed safely. The wooden ramp made no noise of protest nor showed any sign of being unable to bear a man's weight, although its width would force everyone to cross single file.

"It is safe," the sailor said on the other side of the divide, as he stopped to untie the rope. Ziyad had set his torch down upon the black marble floor and re-sheathed his sword to have both hands free to work the tight knot loose.

As the rope hit the floor and began to be rewound by its bearer, Ziyad picked up his torch to await the others.

"Tishimi and Ralf first," instructed Sinbad. "Then our supply bearers. I will bring up the rear behind Henri and Wasif. Be alert for other keys after we cross so our bridge is not withdrawn behind us."

The lone lady amongst them had to sheathe her short sword to accept a now-lit torch from Govad. But as she turned to look across at her destination, Tishimi paused, staring at someone or something past Ziyad.

"What is it?" asked Ralf.

The threat was silent. The sailor was lifted into the air by his unseen foe as the samurai started to yell out a warning.

Ziyad seemed no more than a feather to his attacker, as the light from his torch revealed a suggestion of something huge and bulky behind him. The sailor tried to reach his sword but screamed as if being skewered. Ziyad and his assailant disappeared into the darkness as his torch fell onto the black marble floor.

"I have come to relieve you," announced Hassan, as the sailor climbed up the Blue Nymph's rigging.

"My thanks," said Savas, as he moved to let the new arrival take his place atop the ship's single mast. "All is quiet so far, but with Captain Sinbad…"

"I know," agreed the other man. "This is far from my first voyage with him, but the best part of serving aboard the Blue Nymph is when we return to port and can enjoy the rewards of the voyage," he said with a smile.

A new voice interrupted Savas before he could reply. "Omar wishes to know, what have you to report?" yelled Haroun, from the main deck below them.

"Tell Omar the sea is calm, with clear skies and no ships on the horizon," shouted the sailor. "No sign of the shore party or anyone else."

Haroun wanted to ask if the look out had noticed the plants moving, but did not want to be made fun of or feel Omar's cane upon his back for such foolishness, so remained silent as the young lad raced back with the news, then asked the Master of the Crew, "Should we be worried that they have yet to return?"

"No," said Omar. "It is not even midday yet." Although he had been given no orders on the subject, every man on-board had volunteered to join another shore party and rescue their beloved Captain and crew mates if necessary. But for now, all they could do was wait.

"What do you think might be on that island?" asked Haroun, looking toward the shore.

Omar, watching a sailor swabbing the deck, asked, "Besides the treasure? A skeleton warrior perhaps. Or a tiny princess. Maybe even a jinni, eh?" he said, recalling some of his friend's tales of voyages past. "One never knows until the challenge is faced. Now you best get back to your duties."

"Yes Omar," said Haroun, as he turned to leave.

What the cabin boy failed to report was that the jungle vines had reached the shoreline, and were now starting to cast feelers upon the water.

Tishimi, closely followed by Ralf, raced across the bridge. Samurai and Viking assumed battle positions next to each other, but the only sign of an enemy was Ziyad's torch lying on the ground.

"The creature must be hidden behind one of those columns," said Ralf, noting that there were more of them on this side of the pit-trench, supporting the dome overhead.

"Not necessarily. Many things could be in here with us, using the cover of darkness to mask themselves," Tishimi pointed out.

"I have not seen or heard anything that would give some monster away, yet we are a brightly lit target with all these torches," said Sinbad, crossing the makeshift bridge.

"Then we shall see them first," swore Henri, launching a flaming arrow as he crossed.

The fiery shaft flew upward in an arc until it struck a stone column and fizzled out. All its light revealed was a large empty inner chamber within the rotunda.

"Nothing nearby," commented Ralf.

"Should we be worried….?"

"Then perhaps it hides higher up in the darkness," said Tishimi, studying what little she could see in the faint torchlight.

"Firing any arrow into the unknown would risk hitting Ziyad," complained Henri.

Then, as if to taunt the archer, the group heard the missing sailor scream again.

"I have an idea," said Ralf. He exchanged his lit torch for an unlit one with Govad, who had picked up Ziyad's, before going over to Bedr. Dipping the cloth wrapped end inside the wooden oil cask, the Viking used the torch like a brush to spread the black substance across the edges of his double-sided battleaxe. Ralf reclaimed his torch and then started scouting ahead of the others, now holding a flaming object in both hands.

There was no question of Ralf Gunarson's bravery as the others followed a few paces behind. Tishimi led the way, both swords drawn once more as Sohrab now carried her torch too.

The procession went deeper into the rotunda until Ralf shouted, "Henri, above and ahead of me on the column to my right!"

With that, Henri nocked and released a traditional arrow while Wasif stayed a step back; ready to hand over a prepared shaft from his quiver if necessary.

Although the archer could not see the target, Henri's trust in his friend was rewarded as an inhuman noise indicated the arrow had found its mark.

"Again!" shouted Ralf, as he started swinging both torch and axe at their foe.

Another shaft yielded another unearthly shriek.

"I have to move back," yelled Ralf, as the flame on his axe blades started to die out. "One more, afire this time!"

Henri complied with Ralf's request, as the Viking started walking backwards towards the rest of the group.

Everyone watched the fiery arrow sail through the darkness and find its mark, as a sickening puncture sound echoed within the rotunda.

"It is a spider, but one bigger than any I have ever seen," announced Ralf, as he sensed the remainder of the shore party behind him.

"That beast must feed on those trapped in the pit," theorized Sinbad. Monsters were nothing new to him.

"Does it have a web?" asked Tishimi.

"Not sure. Why?" asked Ralf in return.

"Besides being an additional trap we do not want to get caught in, the web is probably flammable. Setting it on fire would give us more light to fight the beast by," she explained. Her green eyes narrowed as she attempted to peer into the darkness and discover its secrets.

"Can you do that if we distract the beast?" asked Sinbad.

"Yes," replied Tishimi confidently, sheathing her short sword and grabbing the extra torch from Govad.

Sinbad announced his plan and, with some input from Ralf and Tishimi, a strategy was quickly formed.

"Spread a little oil in front of us to create a fiery barrier while Tishimi locates the web," ordered the captain. Bedr quickly obeyed as they heard a skittering-like noise grow closer.

At first, all anyone could see was the weak flame from Henri's sputtering arrow draw near.

Then, as the fire from the oil on the black marble floor grew brighter, a large shape appeared within the darkness.

Henri's arrows had pierced the left half of the creature's multiple eyes. The fire arrow had ignited the shafts of the other two bolts, causing it more pain. Ichor oozed out of the wound.

Although the beast appeared like any other member of its species, this spider was enormous! The end of multi-jointed legs, four on each side, extended outward from its dark-haired body, and slowly propelled the menace along the floor.

The enormous arachnid clacked its large mandibles in anticipation of another fresh meal. All it had to do was bite one of the many prey to inject the digestive juices that would eventually liquefy their internal organs. Then it would drain the victim dry. The others would be wrapped and saved for later.

While wary of the fire, the spider instinctively knew it was just a matter of time before that ended and it would feed.

Tishimi moved silently within the inner circle of the rotunda, using the black marble columns for cover. She walked cautiously, her katana pointed toward the creature, while her body shielded the torch light from its sight. Her ebony outfit provided excellent camouflage in the darkness as she swiftly circled around and behind the largest spider she had ever seen. While the creature was distracted by her friends, Tishimi knew it would turn to attack the instant the beast became aware of her presence.

By the sputtering light of her torch, she soon found her objective. At the base of one column was the desiccated corpse of the missing sailor. Ziyad's lifeless eyes still bore his final horrified impression of mortal fear, and his now paper dry skin had an unnatural color, as if he'd been dead for ages and mummified. When Tishimi looked up, she saw the spider's web was spun across the gap between several support columns, the lower edge of it well above her head.

But dangling within was an even worse menace.

An egg sac! It was woven inside the thickness of the webbing at the top of one of the columns. Not knowing how long until the spider's young would hatch and add to the threat their mother presented, Tishimi waved her torch overhead, but could not reach the webbing to set it afire. Unless she could get Henri's attention for a well-placed fire arrow, she would have to jump for it, a move the spider would likely see.

With a mighty spring and a dancer's lithe grace, she vaulted into the air. The fiery torch managed to touch one spot and a small flame shot up. She moved rapidly toward various key points along the floor, leaping and twisting, trying desperately to ensure that the overall webbing would burn. The fire had to be strong and hot to kill those eggs.

Once she was sure the obstacle within their path was well aflame, Tishimi set the torch down on the ground. She drew her short sword once more and turned to face her foe.

Swords drawn, Sinbad and his companions prepared to face the spider as Henri fired a traditional arrow into one of its front legs. The leg shuddered in response as the shaft pierced its hairy armor and bit into soft parts beneath, but the creature did not move. The arrows within its eye had burned out, their remains fallen to the floor as spent ash, but the barbs were still buried within the damaged area. The beast would not be easy to kill!

The remainder of the shore party had spread out behind the line of fire, with the rope bearers pausing just long enough to set down their burdens before joining the others. Henri and Wasif were behind the rest, with the sailor guarding the archer.

Sinbad looked at Bedr, holding their oil cask, and asked, "Are you ready?"

"Awaiting the signal, as ordered," he replied.

Then, they saw it.

At first, Sinbad was puzzled as to why the flames were so high up, but figured Tishimi had a good reason for starting it in this manner. Then he saw the fire begin to spread. Soon it traversed in all directions behind the spider as the pattern of an enormous web began to burn in the darkness.

"NOW!" shouted Sinbad, as Bedr splashed oil at the dark bulk of the spider.

Some of the black liquid was caught in the dying wall of fire, and looked like one of Henri's flaming arrows as it traveled across to splash upon its target.

The arachnid crawled back a step to avoid being burned, but could not escape the oil completely.

Another dousing was called for before Sinbad signaled Henri. The archer launched a presoaked, but now flaming arrow.

The shaft barely pierced the creature's hide, but that was not its main goal as the oil dampened hairs ignited.

The spider issued a screech of pain as it scuttled away from the shore party, frantically trying to put out the fire by rubbing its front legs over the affected areas.

With that, Tishimi sprang into action.

Anyone who happened to catch a glimpse of her only saw a dark silhouette back lit by the burning spider web, or a glint of her whirling steel blade tips.

As Tishimi raced along the right side of the creature, only the slight noise made by her katana and wakizashi slicing through either air or into monstrous flesh marked her presence.

The beast tried to turn in hopes of attacking its new enemy, but it was crippled by the fire, and Tishimi was faster. By the time she met her opponent face to face, every limb along that side of the spider bore some wound, as its ichor dripped from her swords.

The creature quickly withdrew, ascending a column the best it could without the full use of a couple of legs. There the giant spider writhed in pain as it clung to a length of webbing between two columns that was not part of the burning creation. Its clacking, snapping jaws were still as deadly though, as venom from a creature that size could kill many men quickly. The others emerged from what was left of their dying fire barrier and spread out so it could not drop on more than one of them.

All except Ralf, that is.

"Come down here, demon spawn, and deal with me!" he yelled, brandishing his axe.

As it suddenly dropped, the spider targeted the Viking, the largest of its enemies. That gave Tishimi time to strike again.

Her battle cry heralded a whirlwind of shining blades and thrusting limbs. While Ralf hacked and slashed at the gigantic arachnid, sidestepping and lunging to attack; Tishimi was a blur of motion—striking here, parrying there. She kept the creature busy while the Viking circled for a killing blow; his mighty strength and the heft of his war axe the only things that would cut through the layers of hardened cuticle that made up the creature's large exoskeleton. It was hard as metal, but with a surprising flexibility that crushed inward with dents or dimpling before it split, making it necessary to strike the same spot repeatedly in hopes of doing any damage. This became problematic with a continually moving target.

Gunarson was a seasoned warrior of many battles and Tishimi a well trained samurai, but they were not going to end this on their own. With his own cry of defiance, Sinbad leapt into action, his scimitar already slashing in great curves as he ran at the spider. He danced before it on the balls of his feet with a wicked grin on his face, his eyes alight with the fire of a true warrior. He was daring it to strike back at him, trying to give one of the others a chance for at least a crippling blow.

"This... thing..." Ralf complained between grunts and hefty thumps of his axe hitting the spider's body, "is nearly... *impossible* to pierce. Why is it... so tough-skinned?"

"It is the angle of your attack," Tishimi called back breathlessly, before whirling away in another deadly dance, one step ahead of the lumbering behemoth. "You have to come up from underneath. It has a natural plating on top."

"Now you tell me!" Ralf grumbled. He backed off, tossed aside his axe, and pulled his sword. "Somebody make it stand up and I'll see how it likes a belly rub," he added with black humor, as he assumed a fighting stance, ready to rush in when the moment was right.

The spider had kept its underside turned toward the closest column. Sinbad and Tishimi closed in and pressed the creature backwards, but it was still too low to the ground for the tall Viking to scuttle beneath. "I'd do the honor myself, but I don't think my blade has the strength for the killing strike," she shouted to the others.

"Mine is for slashing, not for pig sticking," Sinbad said irritably. "We need to blind it! Henri..."

"I know what to do, Mon Capitaine," the archer answered. "Give me those longer broad heads from your quiver, Wasif! The ones without the rags," Henri insisted. He nocked the first one and drew a bead on the creature's head as it swayed and snapped its mandibles at the two adversaries trying to corner it. When he had a clear shot, the arrow flew true and pierced another of the spider's larger compound eyes. For just a moment, it reared back and flailed its front legs.

A moment was all Ralf needed. With a wild war whoop, he rushed in and, with his sword thrusting upward, pierced the heaving abdomen of the beast. He ran the sword in as far as possible, showering himself with a rain of foul smelling, sticky and oozing innards. The giant spider convulsed and flopped over sideways as the Viking dove clear, its remaining legs kicking spasmodically until it curled into a ball and lay still.

"Whew. I am glad that is over," said Henri, while wiping his brow.

"Perhaps," replied Tishimi wearily.

"What do you mean?" inquired the archer.

"Spiders, regardless of their size, are territorial. While I have already destroyed this one's egg sac, I cannot guarantee there are not others within this structure. If there is, once they discover this one is dead, another will take its place," explained the samurai, while cleaning her swords.

"Then let us not wait for that to happen," replied Sinbad, before Henri could say anything.

Henri and Wasif gathered what they could reclaim of his spent arrows in case the missiles were needed again. Not all the shafts were immediately reusable, but many could be trued and re-fletched later.

A young Persian who had yet to see his eighteenth year of life, this was Wasif's first voyage away from home, let alone to serve under Captain Sinbad. He had been wondering what life held for him. He could not help feeling proud about how he had handled this assignment so far. *Perhaps when this voyage is over, I can become the archer's apprentice and secure my future on the Blue Nymph.*

"Nobody worry about me!" Ralf complained as he pulled himself to his feet and tried to scrape the stinking mess off his body. He finally gave up and collected his weapons, having to place a booted foot against the spider's stiffening form and tug mightily to free the sword.

"Ouf, you reek! You will need to burn those clothes," Henri said with disgust. Tishimi's nose was twitching and she moved away from the frustrated Viking as he stomped by.

"I don't smell any worse than you after a night of drinking and carousing," Ralf said angrily.

"Let's get back to our purpose here my friends," Sinbad ordered, though he too made a wide berth around the tall man with the gooey stains that had a strong and fetid stench.

With the far lighter oil cask resealed and the coils of rope reclaimed, the expedition went on, single file, deeper into the heart of the rotunda. While the torches provided the only light within the darkness, every instinct told Sinbad that the sun was high in the sky now and would soon begin its lazy western descent towards sunset. This was not a place where he cared to linger after dark.

Tishimi and Ralf took turns scouting just far enough ahead to be the first response against any possible ambush, but their torches and diligence revealed no foes lurking within the darkness.

"She should wear more color. One can barely see her," Henri said uneasily.

"I believe that is the idea," Sinbad countered.

"At least you can hear the Viking," Wasif said quietly. Ralf made a lot of noise when he moved around.

"Yes, and you can smell him even farther," someone else said, and there was nervous laughter all around in the semi-darkness.

They continued traveling in as straight a course as possible, hoping to eventually reach the center of the humongous structure instead of running the risk of bypassing it somehow.

Soon the scouts encountered another pit within the darkness. It was just as wide and deep as the first one, but with one notable exception.

"Odd. There are no bodies within," commented Tishimi, as she cautiously peered over the edge.

"Probably because no one unprepared has made it this far," replied Ralf.

"Whatever the case, let us look for the floor key to expose the bridge we need to cross," said Sinbad.

Soon another grouping of five squares forming a diamond-like shape was found, but when Sinbad pushed the central one with his foot, the resulting noise was different this time.

"No bridge, but metal spikes have appeared from the bottom," announced Tishimi.

"Then let us see what this one does," said Sinbad, as the samurai rejoined them.

As his foot pushed upon the next square in the floor, flames appeared in the pit. The fire rapidly spread outward in both directions, filling the trench.

"There must be oil under this place," commented Merikh, watching the fire burn. "When it is released, something must also create the spark that sets it ablaze."

"And if allowed to burn long enough, it could serve as a funeral pyre to any unfortunate searchers before us," realized Ralf.

The flames would probably have encircled the untraversed section of the rotunda had not Sinbad quickly pushed the square next to the one that released them. Doing this soon extinguished the fire, but a quick look revealed that the metal spikes remained.

"There are two squares left," said Sinbad, looking at the spot on the floor. "One must extend the bridge we need, but what does the other do?"

"Perhaps it removes the spikes," guessed Henri.

"Maybe, but I do not want to discover otherwise," replied his Captain, thinking over the situation. The top two controlled the fire. The center one put the metal spikes in place. If the squares were in order and the next did what the archer thought, then the proper one to touch would be the lower right.

With that, Sinbad was rewarded with the same sound that heralded the appearance of the first bridge.

Their passage secured, the landing party continued deeper into the rotunda.

"Omar! We're taking on water!" shouted a sailor.

"What?" said the First Mate in disbelief.

"The Blue Nymph *is* lower in the water now!" replied the sailor.

The older man took a quick glance over the side and confirmed the observation was correct. The ship did appear less above the sea line now, as if it was carrying more weight.

"Merciful Allah. I feared this voyage was too quiet. I need a team below deck to check for leaks! Start repairs as needed!" ordered Omar.

As men scurried to obey his orders, the Master of the Crew started looking around to assess the situation. The ship was still anchored at the same point Sinbad left it. The carved figurehead of a mermaid, from which the vessel drew her name, was pointed out towards the sea, as if longing to return to her native environment. So if that had not changed…

"We're tight. No damage below deck," came the report moments later.

"Then it must be something else," realized Omar, going to the side railing again. Peering over the wooden barrier, there was nothing amiss port and a quick scan over the other side revealed starboard was clear too.

But aft, a line of wooden tendrils could be seen extending from the island to the ship.

"Where did these blasted vines come from! They're all over the stern and rudder, and are actually trying to pull us down!" shouted Omar.

"What manner of sorcery is this?" one sailor demanded to know.

"What devil has the Captain run afoul of now?" asked another. All seamen are superstitious, and these were beginning to panic.

Without acknowledging or answering their questions, Omar turned to the crew and shouted, "Stop your foolish yammering! I need real men up here, not frightened harem girls! Some of you go on ropes over the side with hatchets and swords to start chopping them away! Free the rudder first. The rest of you, raise the anchor! Maybe the current will help buy us some time. If we have to, we'll hoist the anchor and raise the sail and hopefully, the tide and winds will pull us free."

"If we leave, what about Captain Sinbad and the others?" asked Haroun, fearful of what might happen to him if anyone discovered he failed to warn them about the vines sooner.

Omar rounded on him with a frown. He did not like to have his orders questioned. "My job is to protect this ship and crew, boy. If necessary, we'll come back for them later," he replied.

If we can, he was thinking but did not say.

Sinbad spotted a faint light ahead.

Cautiously, the shore party approached the oasis in the darkness. The light continued to grow brighter until it began to outshine the torches although, leery of anything within the rotunda, nobody extinguished theirs.

At the border between the darkness and the light, before them appeared a ring of black marble support columns encircling the innermost chamber of the rotunda. The pillars were placed far enough apart that the expedition could now stand three abreast between them, and ended at the bottom edge of the golden dome supported overhead.

Dazzling sunlight poured in from a large opening at the very top of the dome far above. That space appeared to be covered by some kind of clear bubble, which kept the inner structure unweathered by the elements. The only other opening within the golden roof was a crude hole matching the one spotted during their scouting of the area before entering the rotunda.

A wide perimeter walkway, composed of many multi-colored yet curved tiles bordered the black pillars and surrounded the open space, which was actually a depression at the exact center of the rotunda. Blackened steps led into that hollowed area, which appeared to be at least as deep as the structure's base.

However, it was what lay within the center that drew the most attention. Several men gasped, as their eyes lit up with wonder and more than a little greed. Before them was more riches than a legion of men could ever spend in their combined lifetimes! Gold, silver, and jewels in unimaginable quantities were strewn everywhere haphazardly; as if whoever was amassing this wealth gave up on trying to keep it organized and settled for just being sure it was all contained in one place.

Sinbad was less awed than troubled. "That statue on the pedestal in the center must be Kumana, but I have no idea where the rest of all this wealth came from," he admitted. "The young Emir never mentioned this treasure, which makes me wonder if he knows about it."

"More important, how did it get here?" Ralf rumbled. He also was uneasy about the heaps of wealth. Its presence felt like the bait of a trap!

"What is that thing?" asked Govad, pointing. There was something else amidst all that amassed treasure, partially buried within the wealth behind the statue. What was visible appeared large, smooth, and rounded.

"It looks like an egg," replied Sinbad after a few moments of deliberation. He was studying the chamber intently, wary of more traps.

"Really?" asked Ralf in disbelief. "What manner of bird could lay something that large?"

"Given its apparent size, it would have to be at least a roc's egg," answered Sinbad. The oval object was an off-white color and, with the distance between them, at least his height in width.

"As long as it does not contain a horde of infant spiders, I care not what is inside," commented Henri.

"I have encountered a two-headed roc before. Yet this egg looks even bigger than the one that foul creature must have hatched from," said Sinbad.

"What are we waiting for?" asked Sohrab, as he set his coil of rope down. His lusting gaze was transfixed upon the treasure as he boldly stepped out onto the multi-colored floor.

"The young Emir never mentioned this treasure..."

The moment his full body weight was past the black marble columns, the man-sized tile he was standing on tipped as the floor disappeared beneath him! Sohrab instinctively reached out to grab the sides of the now open chute before he could fall in completely, but that led to another unfortunate surprise.

The bordering trim of the decorative trap door was razor sharp! The finely honed metal sliced through his fingers, straight to the bone and beyond, as his body weight continued to pull him down. Sohrab's screams of pain and terror echoed upward until there was nothing but a resounding thud as the tile closed behind him through the action of an unseen spring hinge.

It all happened in a heartbeat, with no one able to save him. All that remained of the dead sailor were the bloodied stumps of his finger tips, with no other indication that this one curved tile was anything other than part of the decorative perimeter walkway.

"Allah have mercy!" exclaimed Govad. "What a horrible way to die!"

"Is the whole floor like that?" asked Wasif uneasily, not wanting to proceed into the innermost chamber without some guarantee of safety.

"I do not know," admitted Sinbad, staring at the new trap before them.

"Now that we know what lies ahead, perhaps we should go back to the ship, prepare better, and set out again fresh in the morning," suggested Henri.

"I agree, Captain. There is no dishonor in leaving empty handed today and try again tomorrow, especially after what we have lost," added Ralf, staring at the treasures that were so close at hand.

"I think I have detected a pattern within the floor colors" announced Sinbad. "A black tile took Sohrab's life. There is a multitude of those, alternating with red and white ones, which are probably also traps. But only once every so often is there a blue tile."

"Do you think those form a safe path?" asked Tishimi.

"I shall find out," replied the captain, as he requested a rope be tied around his waist.

Piruz and Ralf held the other end, ready to pull him back to safety when needed, as Sinbad set out.

The first blue tile did not appear until the next row, but he was able to step over the outer circle of tiles with ease to reach it.

As his foot began to touch the space, Sinbad was relieved that the blue tile did not begin to give under his weight.

Now standing firmly on the safe space, he paused only long enough to search for the next blue tile.

That was two spaces to Sinbad's left in the next row. Not extremely difficult to reach, but a stretch to do so without putting any of his weight upon the surrounding tiles.

The zigzag course of blue tiles was taking him closer to his goal as Sinbad easily stepped on the one a space to his right.

However, as he stood on that latest safe space, Sinbad discovered there were no blue tiles present on the final row!

Omar watched intently as the sailors desperately chopped away at the vines that were trying to sink the Blue Nymph. Thankfully, the ship's rudder was easy to rescue for, while not removable, the thing they fought seemed to have no interest in that part of the ship compared to the rest of the aft hull.

"What manner of monster is this?" one man asked, as he continued to hack away at the growth before him. "Every time we cut one of these plant things off the ship, two more takes it place!"

With the sail deployed, what little breeze was present favored them. The bright blue indigo cloth billowed as the vines were drawn tight. Free of the water, their true length and origin point from the sandy shore of the island were revealed, but nothing more. Omar knew that while it bought them some time to continue fighting, the sail alone would not save the Blue Nymph and its crew. Even if the weather favored them now, the breeze would lessen come sundown and the strain of this strange battle could pull the ship apart.

"Keep working at chopping those vines away while the rest of us lighten the ship's weight," ordered the Master of the Crew. "As soon as we do that, more will join you over the side to help."

But as Omar started to turn to issue those instructions, he heard a scream. Looking back over the stern railing, he demanded to know what happened.

"It was a vine!" came the response. "It just wrapped itself around Ahmed's leg, while he was next to me slicing through another branch, and it pulled him under to drown!"

"The last row of tiles are larger than the rest, with no blue one in sight. I need some more slack to jump over them," Sinbad called back to the others.

"Aye captain," was Piruz's reply, as he and Ralf allowed the rope to go limp across the multi-colored tile floor.

Stepping back to the far edge of his last oasis of safety within the deadly sea of trap doors, Sinbad took a running leap, and easily cleared the final hurdle to his destination.

Grateful to still be alive, he turned back to face the others. "I am going to scout the area. Ralf, tie the other rope around your waist and be ready to cross when I call."

"Aye Captain," acknowledged the Viking, as he turned to follow Sinbad's orders.

Not believing the sight before him, Sinbad began to walk through the amassed wealth as if trying to traverse a muddy shore to reach dry land. The trek, while short, was not easy to make. The sunlight pouring through the clear opening overhead made everything sparkle so brightly that he had to squint when glancing downward to check his footing, for solid ground was deep below all the gold and jewels. His legs sank deep into the collected treasure with each step.

Thankfully, there were no apparent traps within the inner circle of the rotunda, but Sinbad was leery of the egg beyond the statue. The beast that laid it was nowhere in sight, and the sea captain had no idea how long they had until either it returned or whatever was inside the egg began to hatch.

Reaching the base of the pedestal in the center, Sinbad looked up from where he was and studied the goal of this voyage. The Statue of Kumana was no taller than he, and looked like any figure of a warrior to him. Made of what appeared to be finely polished stone, it held a curved sword in one hand and carried a shield in the other, with no runes or other distinctive markings upon either it or the pedestal.

Sinbad wondered if it would take more than Ralf and himself to carry the statue back to the Blue Nymph, but a brief attempt to pick it up himself revealed another surprise. The Statue of Kumana weighed far less than stone should. One man alone could heft it easily.

Why would anyone create a hollow statue? I hope this does not bode ill for us, he prayed, before summoning Ralf to cross the deadly tiles.

Soon Gunarson carefully traversed the crooked path of blue tiles before he waded through the amassed treasure to join Sinbad. As requested, the Viking carried the two burlap sacks with him. One still held the old sail, while the other was now devoid of spare torches.

Although Bedr was now holding it, Sinbad had Piruz release his rope so both men could concentrate solely upon keeping the one around Ralf taut. Untying it from around his waist, Sinbad then coiled up that rope and handed it to Ralf. "Wrap up the statue with this and the sail, and carry it out of here," he instructed his companion. "I shall fill the sacks with what I can safely carry of the treasure. The families of the dead need some recompense for their losses."

Ralf simply nodded and both men silently went about their tasks.

But there was one striking detail of note that Sinbad had overlooked. "It looks like something is missing from the statue's helm, as if a jewel has fallen out. Is it anywhere near you?" asked Ralf.

The men searched the surrounding area but found nothing that would fit the empty depression within the center of the statue's helmet.

"We'll never find it in this mess. Let's finish tying it up and leave this cursed place," said Sinbad uneasily.

As Ralf lifted the statue off the pedestal so Sinbad could finish wrapping the old sail around its feet, something inside went 'click'.

The pedestal vibrated slightly as a klaxon within it began ringing loudly.

"I don't like this," Sinbad said unhappily, as something large began to stir within the amassed wealth behind the egg.

The crew of the Blue Nymph jettisoned everything nonessential over the side of the ship's hull. The stone ballast weights went first, tossed onto the vines in hopes that their mass would assist in freeing them. What few empty crates and barrels were available went next. All things that could be replaced upon their next port of call, providing they could break free to sail the seven seas once more.

As the sailors clinging to the side of the ship continued to try chopping it free with their swords, Omar watched with interest as from time to time, a stray tendril would pause to stretch out and feel what was present amidst the strands. After sensing no threat, it would rejoin the rest to continue the attempted sinking of their vessel. Trapped on the vines behind the Blue Nymph, the current could not carry the debris away.

Omar considered sending men ashore to fight the problem from that end, but feared what resistance they might encounter there. Then an idea occurred to him.

"Everyone back on board!" ordered Omar. "We're going to try burning our way to freedom!"

Drawing his double-edged axe, Ralf turned toward the source of the noise and saw a pair of huge, light green eyes with black slits appear within the haphazardly gathered gold and jewels. The orbs assumed a more menacing appearance as a large figure began to rise behind the egg.

"A giant lizard!" someone shouted, as Ralf placed himself between Sinbad and a red scaled object that gradually began to extract itself from the wealth.

The creature stood on four legs to the height of the big man's shoulders, and completely filled the latter half of the rotunda's inner circle to the point that its long tail stretched out onto the multi-colored tile floor, but was too big to be caught in any of the trap doors. It glared at the intruders, shrugging off sleep as the alarm within the pedestal continued to chime.

Thinking quickly, Sinbad began gathering handfuls of the surrounding treasure and started pouring them on top of the pedestal. While some coins and jewels fell off, most stayed in place as the pile began to grow. Working as rapidly as he could, Sinbad only stopped when there was enough wealth amassed to equal the statue's weight, for the klaxon within was finally silenced.

While Sinbad was busy, the lizard extended a long, forked tongue past a mouth full of teeth like curved daggers. The appendage danced in and out menacingly as the beast let out a warning hiss. Eying Ralf and his weapon, it moved closer to the egg.

"It is a Lindworm, and we are within its nest!" the Viking said with awe. "As long as we do not approach it or the egg, we might survive."

"Then let us not overstay our visit," suggested Sinbad, as he began carrying the wrapped statue away.

Ralf kept an eye on the monstrous reptile as they made a hasty retreat. Whether or not it was supposed to be guarding the statue, with its egg safe, the beast made no further move toward the trespassers.

"Can you carry this and make it back across?" asked Sinbad as they drew near the trap doors.

"This statue is not stone, but some kind of metal painted to appear as stone," said Ralf. "Hollow, yet I can find no openings within it. As long as you can hand it to me after I clear the first circle of tiles, I will make it across."

"Very well," agreed Sinbad.

As Ralf crossed to the blue tile in the next ring, Sinbad lifted their prize and moved it toward him. Gunarson easily crossed the rest of the traps safely, carrying the deceptively light statue over one shoulder as Piruz and Bedr took up the slack in the rope around his waist so Ralf would not trip.

With a half full sack slung over each shoulder, Sinbad started out across next. The sleepy beast never moved away from the egg, but hissed at them occasionally.

As the men under his command worked feverishly to prepare for the Blue Nymph's hopeful escape, Omar heard Hassan, the current lookout, shout a warning of something approaching the ship.

He looked up to see the shadow of a winged creature circling high in the sky overhead.

The First Mate yelled to the sailor to come down as the thing began diving towards them; but then felt a heavy, storm worthy gust of wind that knocked everyone above deck off their feet.

Feeling himself pressed against the deck planks by the strong gale, Omar heard a loud splash as something hit the water.

When he could stand once more, Omar saw the tip of the ship's broken mast floating in the water. A quick glance told him that while battered by the mighty blow, the sail, and rigging were thankfully still mostly intact.

Omar was about to order the men to battle positions when he saw the threat flying toward the island, with Hassan struggling to break free of its talons.

Back on the other side of the dangerous floor with the remainder of the shore party, Sinbad was about to give the order to depart when a loud roaring sound heralded the arrival of their next challenge.

"There!" shouted Tishimi, spotting the enormous red figure. It had entered through the crude opening and was now perched on its edge, opposite their position. She had heard about the Ryuu since childhood, but only in folklore and art from her home village and the lands nearby. To discover that they actually existed, let alone be privileged to see one now…

This creature was much larger than she ever imagined. Sunlight glistened through the clear roof section upon the red hued scales of its body. Its great wings were currently folded along its back. The dragon also had two large horns sticking out from the top of its head, marking it as male, and adding even more danger to the already looming threat.

It was looking down at the inner circle of the rotunda, moving its head from side to side sniffing the air.

"Azhdahā?" asked Merikh.

"Ezhdehā!" replied Bedr, pointing upward to where Tishimi was looking.

"Is it really a Bēvar-Asp?" Govad asked Sinbad.

"Or perhaps a Dahāg," he answered.

"It is a dragon," Tishimi informed them.

"Do you think it is aware of our presence?" Ralf asked her.

"The other certainly is, although I do not understand why only one of them has wings," said Henri, with an arrow nocked and ready to fly.

"The winged one is the male," said Tishimi. "He hunts for his mate, and she guards their egg. I have heard stories of such beasts. They never end well for most of the men who encounter them, and our weapons are no match against such a foe."

As the animal near the egg let out a loud cry, the dragon turned to drag out something clutched in a claw. Sinbad recognized the dead face of Hassan, just as the beast above tossed the helpless man down to the lizard below. The creature caught the sailor in its mouth and only the lower half of the dead man's body landed on the surrounding gold.

Several men gasped and whispered prayers for their comrade's soul as a contented rumbling accompanied the sound of tearing flesh and crunching bones. Sinbad watched in mesmerized disgust, his mind racing. Hassan had been a good sailor and was back on the ship, unless Omar had sent him ashore for some reason.

"We should leave before we are discovered," Ralf strongly suggested.

"Yes, let's go now while they're occupied," Sinbad agreed. Although concerned for the welfare of his ship and crew, he was already thinking about possible ways to avoid the creatures and collect more treasure whenever he found himself near this island again and was in need of funds.

Single file, they gathered the torches and began to quietly retrace their steps with Ralf leading the way. Piruz, in the middle of the group, was assigned to carry the coveted statue while Merikh now had the other coil of rope. Sinbad, guarding their rear, only paused long enough to see the dragon rise to its full height before descending to the treasure horde and its mate.

After the wingless beast let out another noise, the dragon moved over to the other side of their nest and stretched out its long neck over the floor trap. Although unable to fully lower its large head to the decorative tiles, the creature leaned forward toward where it sensed prey was. One whiff of the lingering scent confirmed that while gone, it was still nearby. The dragon knew instinctively what to do as it began to inhale.

As they recrossed the second bridge, Ralf Gunarson stopped the procession. He warned of hearing a faint rumbling noise, but it was growing louder.

"Is that beast coming after us?" asked Wasif nervously. He had heard stories from the more experienced sailors about serving under Captain Sinbad, but thought them nothing but wild sea tales, until now.

"If so, it will have to find another route. It is too large for this passage," replied Henri confidently.

They were backtracking through the rotunda and, unless Tishimi was correct about another spider desiring the territory of the one they killed, they found no obstacles in their path. While their combined torchlight did not reveal any new threats present, that did not guarantee one was not lurking nearby.

"Stay alert everyone!" ordered Sinbad. "The noise grows louder, meaning new danger draws near."

Weapons drawn and ready, many eyes peered vigilantly through the surrounding darkness, searching for the danger before it found them.

"Is it just me, or is it getting hotter?" asked Piruz.

What made Wasif look back at that moment as the rumbling noise grew louder, he could not say. But just as he did, the sailor knew that he had to act fast.

Without a second thought, Wasif shoved Henri out of harm's way as he shouted "FIRE!"

Every member of the shore party scrambled frantically in hope of saving their lives as a wall of flame approached.

Tishimi easily sidestepped the lick of fire that tried to claim her life. Ralf, while not as graceful, did the same; although the ends of his long blonde hair were slightly singed.

Govad leapt behind a column, but was almost burned by the fact his jump was slightly farther than it needed to be.

None of the survivors could see each other as the flaming siege continued. They shielded their eyes from the bright conflagration and waited for the fire to die in order to discover the fate of their friends.

Omar began stoking a fire within the ship's brazier while two sailors went below to bring back an unopened barrel of oil and a couple of lead dippers from the Blue Nymph's stores.

As the coals within the metal container began to grow hotter, the Master of the Crew heard the men coming back up the steps. "Put the barrel over by Haroun. He and Raz know what to do."

The men complied with the instructions, carrying their load over to the rear of the ship. Then they watched as the cabin boy broke the barrel's top open with the hilt of his short sword, before he and the other sailor began ladling the oil onto the vines that were still trying to pull the vessel underwater.

"Is everything ready?" asked Omar, approaching with a lit torch in one hand and rags in the other.

"Yes," replied Haroun, as Omar soaked one of the rags in the oil. The cabin boy still felt guilty and remained silent about not reporting the strange vines sooner, but was confident Omar's plan would succeed. He watched as the First Mate held the tip of the soaked rag over the burning torch until it started to catch on fire. With that, Omar leaned over the side railing and dropped it onto the vines, before dropping more flaming rags at different spots. Then everyone watched to see what would happen.

At first, only the rags were aflame, but slowly, the fire began to catch and spread.

Tense moments passed before the blaze started to become stronger. At first, the flames brushed against the outer husks, apparently with no effect.

Then a few puffs of gray smoke appeared as the tendrils menacing the Blue Nymph began to burn.

It was only when one detached itself from the vessel and retreated into the water that Omar breathed a sigh of relief. "It will work, but not fast enough. Man the forward oars and put your backs into it," he ordered the sailors before telling Haroun and Raz to add more oil, hoping to be free before the ship itself was aflame.

As the dragon fire faded and their eyes readjusted to the semi-dark area created by the presence of their torches, Sinbad called out for the others to announce their status.

One by one, the surviving members of the shore party regrouped; save for two.

"Henri! Wasif!" Sinbad shouted as everyone began searching for their missing companions.

"I found them! Over here!" yelled Tishimi. As they approached her position, everyone could see the prone form of the Gaul archery expert lying near the charred corpse of his assistant. "He is just stunned," she announced, while trying to help Henri up into a sitting position on the black marble floor.

"What happened?" inquired Sinbad, kneeling momentarily to address his friend.

"He pushed me out of harm's way just as it was about to rain fire," remembered Henri. "Wasif?"

"I'm afraid he did not survive, but his heroic act will be remembered," promised Sinbad.

"He was a good one; loyal, brave, and smart. He would have made an excellent warrior or sailor. He saved my life," Henri said sadly over the lifeless remains of the young man.

"Then let us honor his sacrifice by getting out of here alive," Sinbad said with a comforting slap to the smaller man's back.

"He pushed me out of harm's way…"

The crew of the Blue Nymph worked feverishly to free the ship from the dangerous, living tendrils.

More oil was poured upon the flames, increasing the conflagration. Yet as each vine released its grip, more took their place, reluctant to give up the quest to sink the ship.

By Allah, when will this end? wondered Omar.

As the flames crackled behind him, Omar checked on the sailors standing by with buckets full of sea water. Another man was below deck. If any sign of fire was spotted there, he would shout the warning, for the First Mate could not let what he hoped would free them destroy their vessel in the process.

Tense moments passed as everything seemed at a stand still. The sailors manning the forward oars strained to move the ship as the acrid smoke from the green and sappy burning material that kept them in place fouled the air.

With watering eyes, Omar watched as the flames crackled higher, threatening to engulf the Blue Nymph along with its unnatural tethers as Haroun and Raz kept applying more oil.

I've done all I can, he realized, looking up briefly to see the sail obscured in the smoke, yet still catching the available wind.

Then Omar turned back toward the stern. Did he hear the snap of a tendril breaking, or was their vessel succumbing to the stress it was forced to endure?

With a sudden lurch, the ship broke the last of its bonds and was free! The slap and roll of wavelets along the sides was a welcomed sound as the First Mate saw their foaming wake increase.

As the sailors cheered their victory, Omar got caught up in the moment of celebration too, before issuing new orders. "Put as much distance between us and that island as possible, while still being able to maintain a look out for the shore party before we drop anchor again. Everyone be prepared to man an oar the moment they return. I also want extra men posted to be alert for either the return of that beast or another attempt by those vines to sink us."

"What do you think Sinbad and the others are facing on shore?" asked Haroun. Raz was now making arrangements to secure the leftover oil as a large red streak briefly appeared above the island.

The creature, presumably the same one that attacked the ship earlier; stood out against the blue of the sky. However, its presence would probably be lost soon within the vibrant colors of the setting sun, for the bottom of the circular sky fire was about to touch the edge of the ocean upon the horizon.

"I know not," admitted Omar, "but knowing the Captain the way I do, we best be prepared for anything."

The shore party, fearing either another fiery attack or the dragon being perched outside and trapping them within, hastily exited the rotunda. Sadly, there was nothing more he could do for the sailors left behind, yet Sinbad did not like leaving the oil cask or extra rope either. He comforted himself with the fact that more could be bought later, as the burlap sacks of wealth pressed against his body, their straps crisscrossed over Sinbad's shoulders.

However, their freedom appeared only temporary as a new obstacle was discovered.

"Our path is gone!" exclaimed Ralf, as they raced to the edge of the clearing. "Somehow, those vines have grown and closed our route here."

"Then we will have to cut and burn our way back to the long boat," said Sinbad. While issuing orders in case the dragon did appear, he stuck his still lit torch within the tangled mass before him as his Persian curved sword began to attack the barrier.

Ralf quickly followed suit on his captain's right, wielding his double bladed battleaxe. Tishimi joined the men on Sinbad's left, her twin swords keeping pace with her shipmates.

Govad kept watch by the statue as the others joined in to help, for it was not long before trouble appeared. "There!" he shouted. "The beast comes!"

"Very well. You know what to do," said Sinbad, not bothering to turn and look behind him.

The dragon had been circling overhead, thinking about attacking the prey on the water as it waited for those within its home to appear. He had discovered this place a long time ago during his travels, and fell in love with she who was now its mate. Instinct told him he could kill the others at any time. It was those below that made the quicker meal.

"Approaching from starboard," yelled Govad. "Its course committed… NOW!"

With that last word, the shore party scrambled away from the vines as the dragon roared and bellowed forth a gigantic blast of fire.

It did not strike its intended targets as they retreated. Instead the flames hit the jungle barrier and burned a deep swatch into the vines as the dragon arched its back to soar overhead. The resulting backlash from such a massive body flying past so fast helped to fan the fire to an even greater degree.

"The dragon's next approach will be from the wrong direction," Tishimi warned, while watching the dragon's flight with more than a professional interest. The animal started to maneuver in a wide arc to return towards the rotunda.

"That is to be expected. A simple matter of common navigation," said Sinbad. "But its course after that will be in our favor again. One more pass, two at the most in the right direction should clear the path back to shore for us," he added, noting how much of the jungle obstacle its flames had burned through already.

But just as the shore party was about to safely flee out of harm's way once more, the foliage lashed out to attempt ensnaring their arms and legs to prevent the dragon's prey from escaping!

Instinctively, they began fighting this new threat. Swords and axe were met by thick tendrils and sharp thorns as each slashed and hacked at their opponents. Sap ran more freely than blood, but both were drawn as the battle continued, until the challenging roar of the dragon grew louder.

"Back into the clearing!" ordered Sinbad. "We'll resume when it flies past."

Unfortunately, not everyone was able to comply.

"Help! I'm trapped!" yelled Bedr. He was frantically using his sword to chop away at a vine around his right ankle even as another tried to ensnare his left wrist.

Sinbad turned to see if there was anything he could do, just as the area was consumed by dragon fire once more.

With no other options, he threw himself to the ground and began to roll his body away even as the great beast cast its shadow over where he stood. A second too late and Sinbad would have found himself trapped within the dragon's claws. The wind gust created by the creature's passing knocked him further away than where he intended, but thankfully Sinbad stopped before thorns could impale his face.

On somewhat shaky legs, Sinbad stood and prepared to fight once more.

His sides hurt from the wealth pushed against him during the tumble, but he was determined to be triumphant this day.

As he prepared to continue the fight, Sinbad saw the dragon turning to attack again.

With the dragon's third pass, Sinbad and company found themselves deeper into the jungle. Another trip in the right direction and the beast's flames would complete a path to the shore. Once there, it would be a simple matter of manning the longboats for their return to the Blue Nymph.

Careful not to be ensnared by the jungle vines as they awaited the dragon's fourth flight over them, the shore party formed a defensive circle to guard each other. It was only when the beast was close that they scattered to avoid either being burned or grabbed. The creature's previous trip overhead had further widened part of the path they stood in, allowing more room to maneuver.

"Here it comes again!" warned Henri, as he spotted the dragon approaching.

"Get ready!" ordered Sinbad, as they prepared to evade it once more.

But as the dragon flew past this time, it did not emit one single ounce of flame! The only danger was from either being grabbed in its massive claws or being knocked down from the force of its passing.

"I suppose it could be either growing wise to our tactics, or else is in need of time to rebuild its internal fire," suggested Tishimi.

"Perhaps we are no longer much of a threat in its eyes and will let the vines deal with us," answered Sinbad, as he watched the beast's form recede from them. "As long as it does not go near the Blue Nymph..."

"Who cares what that thing thinks? Let's just get out of this accursed place," replied Ralf, as he resumed attacking the deadly foliage with his double-bladed battleaxe.

"That might take more time than we have," said Sinbad, noticing the setting sun. "There has to be a way to make the dragon finish clearing the path for us. Wherever it burns the vines, they do not grow back," he noted, commenting upon the areas untouched by flame that were trying to grow near them again.

"Perhaps we can trick it," suggested Tishimi. "In my native land, there are special events where one animal is pitted against another. We just need a creature big enough that the dragon cannot ignore."

I am not going spider hunting, Henri promised himself.

The dragon turned in mid-flight once more, prepared to attack again. The beast knew its flame might not be replenished enough to completely burn its enemies yet, but talon and fang were eternal.

The prey were scattered all about, for something new had appeared amongst them. Deep blue like the water, but breathing fire also.

A challenger? This could not be! The red male dragon roared in anger as he dove down to meet it. He had claimed these two-legged beasts for himself and his mate to feast upon. He fought hard to become the master of this place, and would defeat any usurper that tried to take it from him.

"It is taking the bait," observed Henri, as the dragon approached.

The 'rival' was a hasty creation. The Blue Nymph's old indigo sail that had been protecting the Statue of Kumana was thrown over a section of the thorny vines that still blocked their path. Two torches rested on quickly inserted arrows, the fiery ends opposite each other to create the illusion of flaming nostrils while the arrow barbs appeared as tusks.

The survivors of the expedition watched as the dragon prepared to attack. Ralf stood by the statue, axe drawn; prepared to assume its load as soon as the path was cleared.

What little breeze there was, coupled with the fading light of the setting sun, made it look like another animal was attempting to invade the dragon's territory. The winged beast did as Tishimi predicted and dove angrily for its rival.

With a bellowing roar, the dragon released all the flame it had built up, incinerating the alleged enemy while clearing the remainder of the path back to shore. The winged beast then flew high in the sky, fully spreading its wings in triumph while joyously issuing a victory cry.

As Ralf picked up the statue and their captain resecured the two burlap sacks across his shoulders, Sinbad and company raced to the beach.

The early stars had started to appear in the deepening cerulean of the eastern horizon. But of more importance was that the Blue Nymph, while still visible offshore, was not in its original position.

"I guess they had problems of their own," surmised Govad.

"Probably that winged menace," commented Henri, elated to be leaving.

"Speaking of which," said Tishimi, pointing at the dragon that was flying toward them again.

"Stay away from the longboats! We cannot let the dragon damage them or we will have no way off the island this night," warned Sinbad, as everyone began to spread outward, away from the beast's reach.

The dark shadow of their winged enemy was cast over everything as the dragon swooped down to attack. There was a strangled outcry, cut short before Sinbad felt a gust of wind push him deeper against the sandy ground as the creature flew past.

As the breeze died, he stood and saw the dragon flying back over the jungle towards the rotunda.

Then he noticed the struggling form within the dragon's claw.

Henri said forlornly, "This time it was Govad. The lad was just not fast or lucky enough to avoid the beast's last pass."

The rest hung their heads. So many have been lost on this foul journey!

"It is going back to its mate for the night. We shall be safe until dawn," Tishimi commented quietly.

Sinbad said nothing as he motioned everyone to the longboats.

"The captain's back!" shouted Haroun with glee, as what remained of the shore party scaled the hastily lowered rope ladder.

The crew was happy to see them return, but Sinbad was not in a celebratory mood. "Raise anchor and man the oars if there is no wind left this day," he ordered, noting that the top of the ship's mast was missing and its sail a bit tattered, but still deployed and usable, an interesting sight against the darkening night sky. "I want as much distance between us and that island as possible while it is still safe to navigate. Then we will drop anchor and rest until first light."

"After that?" asked Omar, as he watched to make sure the Captain's orders were being carried out.

"We shall be careful navigating around the whirlpool that guards the way into these waters," began Sinbad, recalling the treacherous passage that almost destroyed the Blue Nymph in their turbulent wake. "At the first opportunity, we shall find safe harbor to make repairs, but we will return to Opres to complete our voyage."

"That thing is what this was all about?" asked Omar, studying the statue.

"Yes, and I want to know what is so valuable about it that cost too many men their lives.

"By Allah! It is wonderful to see you again!" exclaimed the young Emir of Opres, as a guard ushered Sinbad into the public audience chamber of his palace. The sea captain and everyone he brought with him were wearing their best outfits, but were far outclassed by the fine silks their host wore, with a bright ruby centered on his turban.

The Emir dismissed all the members of his court out of the chamber, not willing to share his secret just yet. "Should I consider this a good omen? Did you find what I seek?" he asked anxiously while sitting up more properly on the pile of luxurious cushions his pudgy body occupied atop the dais against the back wall of the room.

"See for yourself," replied Sinbad, as he turned and nodded to Tishimi, who had stayed back by the chamber entrance.

She gave a signal to the guards at the large double doors, who in turn opened the portal in unison.

With a sentry now at either side of the entrance, Ralf pushed a small cart into the chamber. Its platform was cushioned by thick, soft pillows acquired at the ship's last port of call, while a fine cloth covered the object upon it.

The Emir remained silent, his mouth agape in awe as his eyes widened with wonder, not noticing that Sinbad's crew were carefully eying their surroundings. Except for the formal entry way and a private door to the far right of where the Opres ruler sat, there were no other entrances or windows. *Good to know in case Sinbad is right about what we will soon face,* thought Ralf.

The Emir managed to stand up unassisted, although even an untrained eye could tell by the weakness in his legs that it was a task not often performed. The guards paid the proceedings little attention because the visitors had been searched and none were armed.

As Ralf stopped the cart before him, Sinbad said, "It is my pleasure to return to you, the Statue of Kumana," and made a grand gesture of uncovering the prize of their voyage.

The Emir, oblivious to everything else, stared at the object as Ralf lifted it from the cart and set the statue down next to the bottom step of the raised platform.

"I never thought myself privileged to see this within my own life," confessed the Emir, as he walked down the steps to be closer to the statue. "Did you have much difficulty retrieving it?"

"Sea voyages are not without their hazards, but my crew and I never encountered anything we could not handle," replied Sinbad, doing his best to keep the anger about the death toll out of his voice.

"I see," said the Emir, daring to reach out and touch the statue. "Many generations ago, Opres was a troubled land," he continued, never once looking at anything or anyone other than the prize before him. "Would be oppressors and conquerors always plagued us, until the wise men of that age developed a powerful weapon. We were safe then, for no one dared to attack us. But over time, our enemies feared we would conquer them, and so talks of peace began. Eventually, my revered ancestor agreed to hide our most potent weapon in a far away place, where not even he could easily reach it. Since then, Opres and the surrounding lands have been at peace."

Sinbad said nothing but realized that while the Emir's ancestors might have built the rotunda, and perhaps even left the wingless beast to guard the statue, the dragon and spider must have assumed occupancy later. The origin of the living vines might forever remain an unanswered question, but he would never tell the Emir about the other treasure there.

"While peace may bring prosperity, Opres has not been as blessed as our neighbors, and in recent times, some talk of returning to the old ways of war and conquest. But now that you have returned what is rightfully ours, we can protect ourselves and not live in dread of an uncertain future anymore," bragged the Emir, as he removed the ruby from his turban.

As the Opres ruler moved to place the gem within the hollow of the statue's helm, Sinbad nodded for his friends to move closer to the cart. Their weapons were hidden beneath the cushions and might soon be needed.

The red jewel fit perfectly within the open space as a clicking sound was heard. The statue's mouth opened, but nothing else happened.

The Emir waited, thinking it might take time to start whatever he was expecting to happen. However, the statue just stood there with its mouth agape as the Opres ruler grew more impatient. "I do not understand!" he finally admitted. "The legends say that the Statue of Kumana should have come to life under the control and bidding of whoever restored the ruby to its proper place."

"Legends are not always true," observed Tishimi.

"What is that within the statue's mouth?" asked Sinbad, noticing something inside the cavity.

The Emir reached out with a hand bearing many rings and removed the object, before untying the faded red ribbon that was wrapped around a small piece of aged parchment. He stared at it for several silent moments before demanding to know, "What is the meaning of this?"

Sinbad looked over the Emir's shoulder to read the parchment for himself. In faint lettering was only one word: SOLH, the Persian word for peace.

"Your ancestors were much wiser than you realize," explained Sinbad. "They knew that if such a weapon existed, then it could either be stolen and used against them or inspire the creation of even more powerful instruments of war; provided they did not succumb to the lure of such power themselves and use it for more than just defense of their realm."

"But this?" asked the Emir, holding out the parchment with a trembling hand.

"Next to love, peace is the greatest power one can have within their life," replied Tishimi.

"BAH!" said the Emir, crumpling up the parchment and angrily throwing it away from him.

"A calm sea and a pleasant breeze on a warm day or a starry night are always more desirable than any storm," added Sinbad. "Now that the task is done, I shall collect the promised fee and depart."

"What fee?" asked the Emir slyly, in return.

"The one you promised me for bringing the Statue of Kumana back to Opres," replied Sinbad, with a warning edge to his voice.

"I expected you to return with a powerful weapon, not this useless shell before me. There shall be no payment," declared the Emir stubbornly, crossing his arms over his blubbery chest.

"That is too bad," said Sinbad, while reaching under the cushions. In one swift motion, he pulled out his scimitar and pointed it at the Emir. The pudgy man started sweating as he took a step backwards, only to trip over the bottom step of the raised platform.

"I traveled many months and lost seven good sailors on that voyage.

You shall honor your promise, or I shall spread the word as to not only Opres being in possession of the Statue of Kumana once more, but the truth of what it really is."

"You would not dare!" countered the Emir. He thought about calling for his guards, but they were already aware of the situation. However the men were being kept at bay by Tishimi and Ralf, who were now armed too and protecting their Captain's back. While there was a contingent of men waiting outside the palace in hiding if needed, Omar and the rest of the crew were safely on board the Blue Nymph, ready to set sail the moment everyone returned.

"Life is not without risks, yet I know most of mine every time I set sail," replied Sinbad. "My friendship with your uncle was the only reason I undertook this voyage, but he would be ashamed to see the man who rules Opres now." He took a cautious step forward and the pudgy man went pale.

"B-but... I only wanted to make my country richer and more powerful than it is now," pleaded the Emir, staring at the point of Sinbad's sword and wondering what he would do next.

"For Opres, or *yourself*?" Sinbad demanded to know.

"Are they not one and the same?" asked the Emir, blinking rapidly because of the sweat and tears of fear his body was producing, slowly walking backwards away from the menacing figure he now perceived Sinbad to be.

"No, they are not," said Sinbad, shaking his head in disagreement. "As one last favor to the memory of your uncle, we shall talk about that and many other things before my crew and I leave this place. I truly hope you heed those words, for I fear the future of this country under your rule."

"When you do leave, I shall put a price on your head and will take great pleasure to dance on your grave," swore the Emir, for he had reached the secret bell rope at the base of the dais that would summon more guards. He gave it a healthy yank.

Sinbad knew about that rope too and had made sure it was cut at the other end before they entered the chamber. It fluttered to the floor, one end still in the surprised hand of the young Emir.

"Better men than you have already tried, and you see which of us is still among the living," said Sinbad. "Now about that talk..."

The End

My Inspiration...

Before the advent of cable television, many great series and movies of the past could be seen on local stations through syndication. Amongst that vast library were the films of Ray Harryhausen (1920-2013). His body of work in stop-motion animation is unparalleled, and stands the test of time to this day.

A rerun of 1963's *Jason and the Argonauts* was my first Harryhausen experience. While many have commented upon the classic battle with the skeleton warriors; during my initial viewing of the film, I was already awed by the earlier scene where the statue of Talos came to life.

In preparation for writing this tale, I undertook the (guilty) pleasure of watching again all three of the Harryhausen produced Sinbad adventures: 1958's *The Seventh Voyage of Sinbad, The Golden Voyage of Sinbad* from 1973, and 1977's *Sinbad and the Eye of the Tiger.*

With the exception of the giant spider and the living vines, every creature either seen or mentioned within this story has appeared within a Sinbad movie before, but I'm confident that both Ray Harryhausen and Sinbad could have handled those challenges admirably too.

LEE HOUSTON JUNIOR -- is the writer/creator of the HUGH MONN, PRIVATE DETECTIVE and ALPHA the superhero series of novels, published by Pro Se Press. He is also the Editor-In-Chief of The Free Choice E-zine at www.thefreechoice.info ; maintains a professional blog at http://leehoustonjr.blogspot.com , and is an avid reader in what he laughing calls his "spare" time.

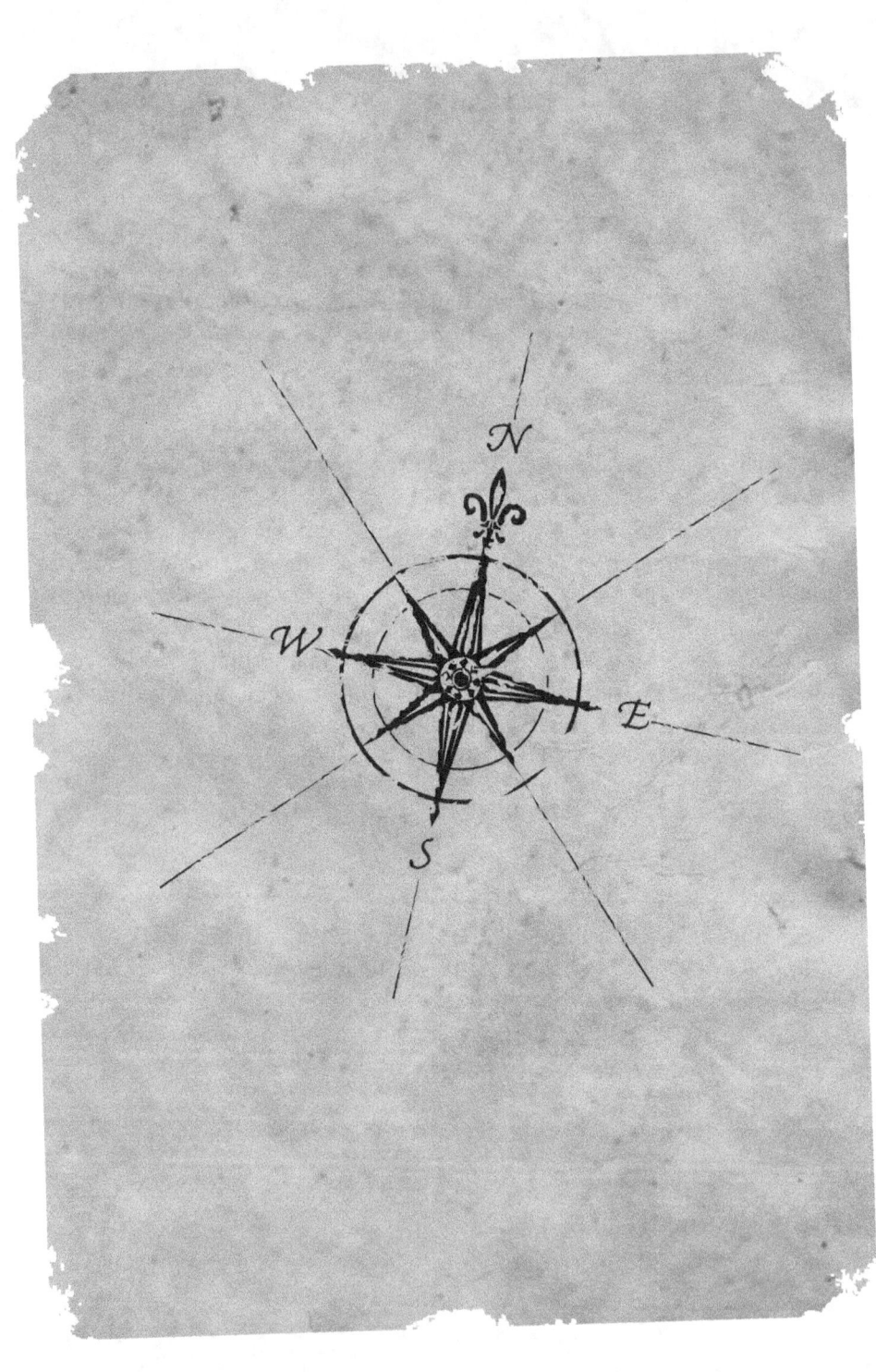

SINBAD and the DEVIL'S SEA

by Percival Constantine

The gray beast stood gingerly on the head of the naked mermaid mounted on the prow of the baghlah ship. Sharp yellow eyes took note of his prey, moving rapidly across the forecastle deck. A tongue snaked out, quickly moistening the predator's lips. He crouched down, muscles tensing and preparing to spring. Claws moved in and out of its appendages in anticipation of the impending kill.

The unsuspecting victim made a sound and with that, the beast sprang forth. He was as silent as he was quick, and the brown rat had not a single second to react as the cat's paw pinned down his pink tail. The feline made short work of the pest and picked it up in his mouth, calmly strolling along the deck of the Blue Nymph. The Persian sailors that made up the crew moved without the slightest consideration to a creature far smaller than them, but the cat had quickly grown accustomed to this. He evaded the stamps and plods with a practiced ease, never once slowing his pace.

The feline stopped in the presence of a large shadow and set the body of the rat down, resting his behind on the ship's Ethiopian teakwood and let out an audible meow to draw attention.

The wide shadow belonged to a short, yet strongly-built Sindhi, who turned at the call. Omar brought himself down to the cat's level, the color of his beard and hair matching his pet's fur. He stroked the cat behind the ears and received a purr of satisfaction in response.

"Good, Samson!" Omar turned his head to the ship's rigging and called out. "Haroun!"

A young man with dark curls hung from the rope-nets connected to the nest atop the ship's mast. He turned, maintaining his grip with just one hand and looking down at the ship's first mate. "What?"

"Come on down from there, monkey!"

Haroun rolled his eyes and let go.

"Not like that!"

Haroun only fell a brief distance before grabbing hold of a fresh bit of rope. He dropped from here, landing harmlessly on the deck. He patted Omar's shoulder and flashed him a white grin. "Relax, you're becoming a woman in your old age."

Omar frowned. "If the Lady hears you talk like that, she'll have your head for a turban."

"Lucky for me she wears none," said Haroun. "Now, what is so urgent?"

Omar pointed to the rat. "You see this? You told me you'd gotten rid of all the rats."

"I did!"

The first mate arched his brow. "So Samson has caught what, then? Is it not a rat?"

"Omar…"

"Or maybe it is the spirit of a rat! Left chained to the place of its death!"

Haroun huffed. "Ahmed said he got them all."

Omar grunted, placing his fists on his hips. "Ahmed is incapable of finding the whiskers on his own chin. I asked you to find the rats."

"I'm sorry, Omar. But I had more important orders."

"More important? I'm the Master of the Crew, what order trumps mine in terms of importance?"

"His." Haroun pointed to the quarterdeck. Easily controlling the wheel of the ship with a single hand was the captain. A tall man with an athletic build that would make the statues of Greece turn emerald with jealousy. His skin was as brown as fresh coffee, and the smooth black beard was neatly trimmed and restrained to the area around his broad grin. In sharp contrast to the darkness of his skin and hair were eyes the color of the bluest sea, and every bit as mysterious.

Haroun faced Omar with a smile. "You would not have me disobey the command of Sinbad El Ari, would you?"

Omar grunted. "Get back to work."

Samson made a protest with a louder, somewhat insistent meow. Omar sighed. "Yes, yes, I will get you your fish. Come, let us see if the morning catch has anything."

An Arab ship and warm climate would be the last place one would expect to find a veritable mountain that walked as a man, but that is what the Blue Nymph had in the form of the young Viking warrior, Ralf Gunarson. He dragged the broadsword along the grindstone, sharpening the edge for battles he hoped they would soon find themselves in the midst of. Seated near the Viking was Henri Delacrois, the far slimmer and shorter Frenchmen, affixing fresh heads to the wooden shafts of his arrows. Ralf hefted the broadsword in both hands, holding it at an angle to give him a keen view of the blade. He blew loose shavings from its edge, admiring his handiwork. The man-mountain gave the sword a few test swings and smiled.

"This is what I do not understand about you archers. Why attack from a distance when the true thrill of the battle comes from locking eyes with an opponent?"

"I prefer a quick, clean kill. Why draw unnecessary risk to yourself?"

"Because that is the way of a warrior, Frenchman!"

"I pity you, my large friend. True pleasure comes not from the heat of battle, but the heat of passion."

"Then it would appear you are on the wrong ship." Ralf set down the broadsword and stroked his yellow beard, giving a snicker. "Unless there is something you have neglected to tell us."

"The images your filthy Viking mind conjures," said Henri with a shake of his head. "I just wish to be prepared for this voyage."

Ralf procured the ten-pound battle-axe from beside the broadsword. He pumped the pedal on the grindstone and brought the axe's edge to the spinning wheel. "You sound worried."

Henri finished assembling another arrow and inserted it into the quiver. The edges of his lips moved his thick, brown mustache around in thought. "The word is cautious. What Tishimi has told us of this place fills me with a certain sense of dread."

"Calm your nerves, friend Henri!" said Ralf, sharpening the axe's edge. "We are in the company of the finest warriors to sail the seven seas!"

"All the more reason to be cautious." Henri held up the arrow, staring at the head as he spun it between his hands. "Even the bravest warriors must meet their maker. You may wish to barrel down the gates to the next world, but I intend on living a long and healthy life."

"Then remain behind on the ship. The rest of us shall claim the glory and the tales as our own!"

The man from Gaul stared at Ralf as if that were the most ridiculous statement he could have uttered. "And miss the opportunity to impress the Lady with my skills?"

Ralf scoffed. "Tishimi has seen your skills. Very little appears to impress her."

Henri twirled the arrow between his fingers before tossing it into the quiver. "My dear boy, you have much to learn of the game of seduction. The Lady Tishimi is a woman, and like any other woman, she shall soon succumb to my charms."

He rubbed the edges of his mustache. "You see, a woman has certain needs, just as a man. And Tishimi is a woman of refined taste. So it is simply a matter of time before her desire takes hold and she runs into my arms."

Ralf had a knowing smile on his face as he gave a nod. "You think so?"

Henri chuckled. "Oh, I know so. Stay by my side, boy. Despite your brutish nature, in time I can transform even you into a man the maidens throw themselves at."

Ralf cocked his head back slightly, looking past Henri's shoulder. "What say you, Tishimi? Think I can one day be a master of seduction on par with the archer?"

Henri's jaw dropped and his blood froze. He carefully turned so he could look over his shoulder. And there, standing in her black silks, was Tishimi Osara. The beauty from the Far East had piercing eyes the color of emeralds and her raven, long, silk tresses were tightly affixed in a bun. Hanging from her waist was the scabbard and inside, the mystic blade she wielded. Her left hand gripped the top of the scabbard and with her thumb; she pushed up on the cross-guard. A bit of the blade's steel was exposed and with a slight flick of her wrist, the sun flashed off the metal and into Henri's eyes. The blade fell back into the scabbard and she turned from the Europeans, walking along the deck.

Ralf patted the nearly comatose Henri on his shoulder. "I think she likes you."

William Byrne walked about below deck, scratching his red beard. The movement of his bullish frame caused the clatter of the glass bottles that the elder attempted to work with. Rafi, the Greek-educated medicine man, huffed his annoyance.

"If I'm to finish my work, I must ask you to sit still. You may not be as large as the Norseman, but your heavy footfalls combined with the rocking of the ship make a delicate matter even more difficult to complete."

William stopped and leaned against the wall, watching Rafi at work at his bench. "My apologies."

"You seem uneasy," said Rafi.

"It is this quest. I wonder what purpose it serves."

Rafi gave a shrug. "Excitement, treasure. The usual things adventurers such as those among the Blue Nymph seek."

The Scotsman did not appear satisfied with this answer. Rafi watched him out of the corner of his eyes. The old man possessed wisdom that extended beyond his knowledge of medicine and language. "Although perhaps that is not what some seek."

William gave a startled look to Rafi. A moment's pause was followed by a laughter that was slightly nervous. "Not at all. I…what I mean is that I just worry if this treasure exists. We are going on nothing more than a half-remembered legend from a woman's childhood."

Rafi dropped some herbs into a small mortar and crushed them together with the matching stone pestle. "So your concern is simply related to the truth of the legend?"

William nodded. "Of course. Why else would I be concerned?"

Rafi turned on his stool and gazed at the large Scotsman with a knowing smile. "As you wish. Just remember that the tongue may say as it pleases, but the eyes never lie."

"I don't know what you mean."

"What I mean, my friend, is that your bravado may convince the crew that you are simply another adventurer. But both you and I know you feel you have a far nobler purpose aboard this vessel, one that extends beyond simple wealth and glory."

William huffed. "You gleaned all that from my eyes?"

"Mmm."

"Then Rafi, perhaps your eyesight is fading with age." William stepped away from the wall and moved to the steps, heading to the main deck. Rafi continued to work on preparing ointments and balms that would prove useful to the crew when they went ashore.

"To each his own, my friend."

Tishimi kept her grip on her sheathed blade as she walked about the Blue Nymph. For the young warrior, it had become a habit to be prepared for danger at all times, so she could react at a moment's notice. She could feel the eyeballs of some of the crew glued to her form…for some, it was out of a superstitious belief that women should not be allowed onboard. For others, it was something more unseemly. But none would dare to even consider speaking ill of her. Although they may claim it is for fear of the Captain's reprisals, in truth it was fear of Tishimi's unparalleled skill with her blade.

She walked with a silent confidence across the surface, climbing the wooden steps up to the quarterdeck. Sinbad held the wheel, controlling the movements of his ship with one strong hand, his dark blue eyes gazing out over the horizon.

"How do we fare?"

"We have passed the lands of the Barangay and soon we shall enter the Ma no Umi."

"The Devil's Sea?"

Tishimi allowed a small smile at the translation. "Your studies are coming along, I see."

Already proficient in several languages, Sinbad was intrigued to learn more. Since Tishimi joined the crew, it provided the accomplished sailor with an opportunity to learn the Japanese language under her tutelage.

"These waters are rumored to be extremely treacherous for any vessels daring to enter. For that reason, I believe here we may find the lost kingdom of Yamatai."

"And the treasure we seek?"

"Yes, the treasure of the Sun Queen." Tishimi gave a sighing nod. "I don't suppose any further attempts to dissuade you from this fool's errand will bear fruit?"

His grin widened. "Sinbad thirsts for adventure, always! You cannot tell a story of rare treasure hidden within dangerous waters and expect him to let the opportunity pass!"

"If the legends of Himiko's power are true, then we can expect quite a difficult path ahead of us. The Devil's Sea has claimed all who enter its territory. It is said that even in death, Himiko defends her treasure."

"Good!" said Sinbad. "If there were no danger, it would not be worth the effort!"

"Captain!"

Sinbad heard the call come from above and he turned his eyes to the rigging. "What has Haroun's keen eyes spotted?"

Haroun pointed off to the right. "Wreckage ahead, off the starboard!"

"Shall we see what sort of calamity awaits us?" Sinbad did not wait for Tishimi's response, spinning the wheel so he could reposition the ship on a path with the wreckage.

"Be ready for anything," said Tishimi. "Your thirst for adventure may one day be your end, Sinbad El Ari."

"Ah, and what a glorious death that would be!"

Under Sinbad's experienced use of the wheel, the Blue Nymph moved closer to the wreckage. It was a smaller vessel, definitely constructed in the oriental style, but it had run afoul of an islet that broke through the hull. The crew of the Blue Nymph threw hooked ropes across to anchor their ship to the damaged one.

Despite Tishimi's reluctance to pursue this quest, she was nonetheless the first to swing from a rope affixed to the mast. She released at the apex of the swing, nimbly flipping in the air and landing so gracefully on the wreckage that she may as well have been floating. Sinbad tugged on the harness that kept his scimitar tied to his back and followed her over next, with Henri at his side. William took hold of a rope and followed them, but as Ralf prepared to follow his crew-mates, he heard the protests of the first mate.

"Are you mad, you stupid oaf?" cried Omar. "Your bulk is likely to bring the mast down upon our heads!"

Ralf rolled his eyes. "Oh very well." He released the rope and backed up, then charged toward the ship's railing. On his approach, he planted a foot on the rail and sprung forth from it, the strength of his leg muscles overriding gravity's hold on his large frame. Ralf landed on the deck of the oriental ship like a cannonball, one of his feet breaking through the wood.

"So this is the threat of the Devil's Sea?" asked Henri. "A beached ship? I've had former lovers capable of more violence than this."

"We shall attempt to conceal our surprise," was Tishimi's dry response.

Sinbad chuckled. "All jest aside, Henri's words are not without merit. A ship that has run afoul of an islet is hardly cause for concern."

"Assuming that's all it was." William's nose scrunched and he brought a hand to cover his mouth and nostrils. "The stench is foul."

"The stench of death." Sinbad gave voice to the odor that assaulted them, but he simply confirmed what these battle-hardened warriors had become familiar with long ago.

The deck was littered with around a dozen bodies. Their eyes were open, faces frozen in expressions of absolute terror. Henri kept as far from the bodies as he could, practically dancing around them as he moved across the wooden planks. "This all came from striking an islet?"

"No." Sinbad addressed Tishimi. "They all wear similar clothing. Do you recognize the uniform?"

Tishimi nodded without meeting her captain's gaze. "They are the oryoshi, warriors who serve the imperial court of Japan. But if they dared venture into the Ma no Umi, that suggests they too sought the treasure of Himiko."

"And were killed for it," said William.

"Search the ship, find anything that may grant us more insight," said Sinbad.

The boarding party obeyed their captain's order, spreading out among the deck. Henri approached one of the masts, which had been split apart. The bamboo sails were torn and shredded, but there was no indication that the islet itself was responsible for this damage.

Ralf ascended to the quarterdeck with Sinbad by his side. At the rear of the deck lay what they assumed was the captain, pinned under the ship's wheel. Ralf bent down and hefted the wheel from the body as Sinbad examined its former mount.

"Its weight is not insignificant, Captain," said the giant.

"Aye, appears it would have taken some force to separate it," said Sinbad. He stepped to the ship's railing, resting his hands on the edge and looking out into the darkened seas. "A storm appears to be brewing."

Sinbad felt a vibration against his abdomen. He stepped back from the railing and looked down. In his sash was a six-inch dagger with a jewel-encrusted blade. The Grachene, given to him by the goddess Persephone, that has a habit of vanishing on Sinbad. Its presence could only mean danger was imminent.

"Allah preserve us…"

On the main deck, Tishimi approached the doors of the captain's cabin. She tried to push and pull, but they would not budge. William stepped forward. "Would you like me to tr…"

Tishimi didn't allow him to finish his request, forcefully kicking the doors and breaking them open. She glanced at him. "I'm sorry, you were saying something?"

William sniggered. "I suppose not."

Tishimi entered the cabin, her hand prepared to draw her blade. What she found was another of the oryoshi, prone over a table, arms spread…. as if he were trying to protect something. William grabbed the back of the corpse's uniform and pulled him away, allowing him to drop lifelessly to the ground. Tishimi examined what the man died protecting. There were various scrolls with characters that the Scotsman had never seen before in his life.

"What are these?"

"Kanbun. Many official documents are written in this."

"You can read it?"

"Of course." Tishimi ran her finger along the characters, which were written vertically from right to left. "They talk of the legend of Himiko and the land of Yamatai. No real knowledge that I don't already possess."

William thought he heard something. He turned his head and cast a glance through the doors. He saw Henri wandering about the deck, examining some of the bodies and lifting whatever small treasures he could find. But nothing out of the ordinary. William's eyes drifted to the dead man who lay by the open doors, but his lifeless, terrified eyes just stared vacantly back.

Tishimi was careful as she shuffled through the parchments, taking quick assessments of whether or not it was useful to their quest. There beneath the scrolls, she found something that did catch her interest. "This is what we need."

Her statement briefly took his attention from the corpse. "What did you find?"

"A map." She made room for him to step closer to the table and view the map himself. He scratched his red whiskers while staring at the illustration.

"I don't understand, we have maps like this."

"No, it's…" Tishimi looked at William, but her words died and her eyes enlarged. She grabbed the Scotsman and used all her strength to pull him towards her, and the two fell backwards. Before William could express his surprise, he heard the groans of the dead. The corpse had come to life and would have attacked William had Tishimi not acted quickly.

The two warriors quickly returned to their feet. William brought his sword to bear, thrusting it inside the creature. The undead thing hesitated, his eyes housing a bright red glow. He gripped the blade with hands, his fingers elongating into sharpened points, and slid his body off the metal.

"What madness is this?" asked William.

Tishimi moved round the table and jumped on it, drawing her sword just as she pounced at the walking corpse. He stepped back from her, her steel tasting his undead flesh. Not even the blood oozing from the wounds would deter the creature. He howled and dove towards her with the clawed fingers outstretched. Tishimi ducked and pushed forward, throwing her shoulder into his torso and flipping him over her head onto the table. She spun around and her sword fell, severing the creature's head, and dark blood poured onto the floor.

"Don't bother with the body, attack the head," she told William.

A wail of death came from behind. The two warriors spun towards the entrance to the cabin to see another corpse rushing towards them. But an arrow emerged from his forehead and he stopped, falling at their feet. Across the deck Henri stood, notching a fresh arrow. Tishimi and William left the cabin, meeting the archer on the deck. The sounds of battle came from above, where both Sinbad and Ralf sparred with a pair of the undead creatures.

Sinbad ducked the swipe of the beast's claws and lunged forward, shoving the Grachene up through the corpse's chin, driving it into the hilt, then pulling it out. Ralf raised his axe and with a bellow, brought it down upon the head of another corpse, cleaving him into two halves. The three on the deck joined their captain and the Norseman on the quarterdeck.

"What are these things?" asked Sinbad.

"The claws and eyes suggest they are jikininki," said Tishimi. "But something is wrong. Jikininki are like ghouls, they only consume the flesh of the dead. Why would they attack us?"

"Whatever they are, let us thank the gods that we finally have some fair sport on this journey!" said Ralf.

"Speak for yourself, maniaque," said Henri.

The remaining jikininki gathered on the deck, numbering less than ten. The skies were growing dark and it made the crimson hue of their eyes against their yellowed flesh all the more unsettling.

"Come!" Sinbad ran to the edge of the quarterdeck and mounted his foot on the railing, using it to push himself into a leap. With his scimitar in one hand and the Grachene in the other, he landed right in the fray of the beasts, impaling and slicing into them without giving quarter.

Tishimi and William followed their leader without question, mirroring his jump. Ralf charged down the steps from the quarterdeck, rushing like a bull into the midst of the jikininki. Henri, on the other hand, preferred strikes from a distance. He drew and fired arrows with uncanny speed, and rare was it that he missed his mark.

Tishimi moved with extreme grace. She evaded the attacks of the jikininki then returned with strikes of her own from both the short and long sword. Her movements were such that it was as if she were performing a dance.

Ralf was the complete opposite. Whereas Tishimi had smooth grace, he had brute force. He tore into his enemies with such wrath and in such close quarters that more of their blood struck him than the ground.

William was more reserved. He maintained a calm demeanor even under the stress of battle. In contrast to Ralf, he did not relish the call of battle, but more saw it as something that must be done. His heavy broadsword nonetheless never failed to separate head from shoulders whenever one of the jikininki came within reach of his blade.

When the battle ended, the blood of the corpses had stained the wood of the Japanese ship. The crew of the Blue Nymph stood victorious, panting and bodies slick with the sweat of battle. Sinbad looked down and noticed the Grachene had vanished on him yet again. He sighed and slid the scimitar into the scabbard on his back. "Appears the danger has passed."

"Blast…" muttered Ralf.

Henri hopped onto the quarterdeck's railing, perched much like a bird and looking down at his companions. "What now, Sinbad?"

"We have a clue," said Tishimi. She sheathed her blades and ran into the cabin. A moment later she emerged, holding the rolled-up documents and map in her lithe hand. "However, I suggest we return to the Blue Nymph to examine them."

Sinbad nodded his agreement. "Indeed. This ship appears to be of little use to us now."

...he landed right in the fray of the beasts...

The crew salvaged what little supplies were still present upon the oryoshi ship, including some bottles of sake that Henri and Sinbad in particular were quite pleased to discover. Once they returned to the Blue Nymph, Ralf preceded to entertain the crew with the tale of how he single-handedly defeated two dozen of the jikininki. Henri quickly reminded Ralf that there were barely a dozen of them in total, but the giant accused him of ruining a good story. William remained apart from the crew, standing watch at the fore of the ship for any dangers, as did Haroun from his perch high up.

For Sinbad, Tishimi, Omar and Rafi, however, business came before pleasure. They gathered in Sinbad's cabin, and Tishimi explained the documents, translating and summarizing the Kanbun for her mates.

"Centuries ago, there was a land called Yamatai. After the death of their ruler, there was a period of great disorder. That all changed when a woman named Himiko came. She was a great sorceress and she brought the people under control through powerful magicks. Upon ascending to the throne, she was rarely seen, but her power held sway over her subjects. Her rule was so strict it was virtually a slave state. Very little is known beyond that. However, it is said that Himiko possessed a vast treasure. It is said if one can discover Yamatai, the treasure will be theirs."

"Don't we know all this?" asked Omar. "It is the same story you told Sinbad, yes?"

"It is, what new information have you discovered, Tishimi?" asked Sinbad.

"This." Tishimi unrolled another scroll. This one was a map of the seas of Japan. Omar, Sinbad, and Rafi all leaned in closer to inspect the illustration and Rafi was the one to speak first.

"Is this not simply a map of these waters? Do we not already possess this?"

"There is more." Tishimi pointed to some Kanbun characters and circled the sea with her finger. "This is the Ma no Umi, where we currently are. But look here, right in the center." She pointed at a land mass. "No map of these waters I have ever seen, either from Japan or other areas, contains this island. It is a unique feature to this map."

Sinbad stood upright and placed his hands on his hips. "You believe this is Yamatai?"

Tishimi nodded. "It stands to reason. The imperial court must have found this map and sent the oryoshi to investigate. But I still do not understand what happened to them."

"You called them something. Jikininki?"

"Mm. It is said those who had exorbitant greed in life will walk the earth as jikininki after death, cursed with an insatiable hunger for the flesh of corpses. Yet these came for us, which suggests there is a larger power here controlling them."

"You believe it to be this Himiko, do you not?" asked Rafi.

"I'm uncertain," said Tishimi. "Himiko is said to be dead, but if the legends of her power hold any weight, then she may have managed to avoid the next world."

"So we venture on," said Sinbad. "We brave the waters of the Devil's Sea and we locate this island, see for ourselves whether or not it is truly Yamatai."

That night, the crew enjoyed the spoils of their victory over the cursed beasts that had once been the oryoshi. They feasted on the rice they found on the ship and drank hungrily of the sake, passing the bottle amongst themselves as they shared songs from their homelands.

William kept himself separate from the crew. He remained on a constant vigil at the fore of the ship, watching the clouds in the night sky with his emerald eyes. Even with his keen senses, he could not detect the soft footsteps of Tishimi and he gave a start when she spoke from behind.

"You do not wish to join the festivities?"

William calmed himself and gave her a half-hearted smile. She held two small cups, both of them filled with the clear liquid, and offered one to him. He took it with a nod of thanks.

"I am not one for gatherings," he said.

"Nor I."

He took a ginger sip of the drink, testing its taste on his tongue. He gave a smile of satisfaction and took a longer sip. "Not bad."

"It should be drank hot. But I am satisfied simply to have any sake to drink, regardless of temperature. This particular brand is good stock. Nothing but the best for the Emperor's loyal vanguard."

"What do you think we will find out there?" asked William.

Tishimi took a sip of the sake while pondering her words. "I do not know. But I fear it will be far more dangerous than Sinbad believes."

"You think him overconfident?"

"Iie, I simply feel his thirst for adventure sometimes outweighs his better judgment."

But that is why we have all joined this crew, is it not? The pursuit of adventure?"

"For some, perhaps." She directed her stare at William's face. "What of you, William Byrne? You do not seem like the type to sail with a crew such as this."

"The same could be said of you, Tishimi Osara."

"Ah, now this is what Sinbad likes to see!"

The pair turned at the sound of their captain's voice. Sinbad approached them with a cup in one hand and the other holding one of the sake bottles, with Henri by his side. The Frenchman appeared to have already drunk more than his fair share, as his gait was slightly wobbled and his eyes glazed.

Sinbad stepped closer to William and raised the bottle. "Come, my friend. Allow me to give you a refill."

Despite the amount of alcohol he'd already consumed, Sinbad still appeared somewhat unaffected by it. He was able to expertly fill William's cup with one hand, never spilling a single drop. The captain then offered the bottle to Tishimi.

"Will the lady honor us by sharing a drink?"

"I suppose one more." She held out her cup and Sinbad poured her a fresh drink.

"A toast." Sinbad raised his glass and the others followed suit. "To the fair Tishimi. Even if this quest proves for naught, at least we have obtained some fine brew!"

The four touched their glasses together and then drank freely. Henri pushed closer to Tishimi, his breath hot on her neck. "If it pleases, perhaps I can show my gratitude in private?"

Tishimi caressed the Frenchman's face with her soft hand, pulled it away, and smacked his forehead. Henri's head rocked back, and he was more in shock than pain by her action. He rubbed the spot where he'd been struck.

"A regretful decline would have been sufficient..."

"My apologies, Henri. But any decline to your advances would not be regretful," she said with a smile.

Both Sinbad and William burst into laughter and Henri's cheeks brightened in embarrassment.

"I suppose the charms of the French are lost on the Japanese!"

The next morning, the crew fought their hangovers from the previous night and managed to make it up to the deck when Sinbad had commanded them. The anchor was hoisted, the sails dropped, and the Blue Nymph pushed forward into the Devil's Sea. Sinbad commanded the wheel, his blue eyes fixed into the distance. Although none spoke of it, all noticed the skies were far darker than usual at this time of day. The clouds as well began to gather and thunder sounded in the distance.

A storm was coming, and no one aboard was more keenly aware of that fact than Sinbad himself. But still he pushed ahead. His hope was they could outrun it or that it would pass quickly. Even as the wind picked up, Sinbad pushed on ahead, refusing to stop. The claps of thunder were now fewer and fewer apart, and the clouds continued to darken.

Rain began to fall and the waters roughened, angered by the strong winds. Sinbad held firm to the wheel, pushing on into the growing darkness. The storm was upon them now and he would have to fight against the torment.

Sinbad took secret satisfaction in this turn of events. He enjoyed testing his mettle against Mother Nature. The two had clashed many times, and at points Sinbad had been beaten down by her strength. But still he persevered. There was no greater thrill for this sailor than the knowledge that he had gone up against the worst that the elements could throw against him, and still emerged victorious.

The waters were rough. Strong waves lifted the Blue Nymph and Sinbad steered into them when he could, riding them if possible. All aboard the deck were now soaked by the rain, which had come down stronger and fiercer than before. Their clothes clung to their skin like leeches, and some men felt more comfortable in stripping their shirts entirely to move about with more freedom.

For Sinbad, this was validation of their quest. Such rough weather appearing out of nowhere was surely the result of powerful forces working against them. Himiko or whoever guarded her treasure was trying to keep them from reaching the island. That explained the oryoshi who had been transformed into jikininki, and the current weather. This convinced Sinbad that the island was indeed Yamatai, and there were forces attempting to prevent them from obtaining the treasure of Himiko.

"Captain, port!"

At Haroun's shout, Sinbad looked to the left and saw a massive wave rising up, determined to swallow the Blue Nymph whole.

"Hoist the sail!" shouted Sinbad, as he spun the wheel, turning the bow towards the wave. The beautiful mermaid carved into the prow, with her crystal-blue glass eyes, faced the approaching tsunami with the same indifferent stare she gave to any approaching calamity. The wave crested, prepared to descend upon the Blue Nymph with all the force nature could muster.

"HOLD!" called Sinbad, and the crew braced themselves as the Blue Nymph punched through the rising tide. Sinbad pulled his body tightly to the wheel, holding it as still as possible. The wave crashed down, water rushing along the deck. Some crew members nearly fell into the abyss of the ocean but the quick actions of their shipmates saved them from the torment of being crushed beneath the unforgiving waves of the Devil's Sea.

The weather began to clear up. It seemed they had faced the worst of it and come out on the other side. Sinbad laughed, his mood cheerful for their good fortune. Rays of light broke through the clouds and Sinbad raised his arm to welcome them. "Praise be to Allah!"

Omar appeared by Sinbad's side, but his demeanor was far less jubilant. Sinbad slapped his first mate on the back. "You see, my friend? Sinbad's skill once again saves us from the jaws of death!"

Omar grunted. "If not for Sinbad, we would not be on this fool's errand to begin with."

Sinbad laughed at this. "Ahh Omar, your surly attitude will guarantee that you outlive us all."

"Only if I escape this ship…"

From his perch on the mast, Haroun gazed out. With the storm having broke, he could now see clearly into the horizon. And what he saw brought a wide grin to his face. "Land! Captain, we've found it!"

Sinbad smiled at Haroun's words. "Drop the sail!"

The sky-blue sails of the Blue Nymph fell, catching the wind and pushing the ship towards its destination. Sinbad was pleased at these turn of events. They had braved the dangers of the storm and now, they were close to their goal. Nothing could stop them now.

The Blue Nymph came as close to the island as it could before the water became too shallow. A party consisting of Sinbad, Tishimi, William, Ralf, and Henri boarded a small rowboat and departed for the island, with Omar left in command of the Blue Nymph. Ralf's strength alone was enough to provide enough force to row the boat towards the island, and Sinbad stood at the fore, grinning the entire time as they came closer to the beach.

The boat ran aground and they disembarked, plodding through the water until they reached dry land. The sand of the beach was of such a pure white, it almost resembled snow. The sand ended shortly and led into a grassy, forested area. Henri looked up to the skies and noticed a strange hue to them. They weren't dark, but they also weren't light. Instead, they were somewhere between the two. "Are you certain this is a wise course, Sinbad?"

The Nubian borne captain also gazed up at the skies. "I would say without a single doubt that we are in the right place."

"I don't doubt that, only whether this quest is worth it," said Henri.

"You worry too much, Henri," said Sinbad. "Come, let us press on."

They began their trek from the beach, moving into the forest. As soon as they entered the cover of the trees, the darkness that followed suggested that dusk was soon approaching, regardless of the fact that it had barely been noon when they landed. The sun should have been at its brightest, but in this place, the traditional rules appeared to no longer apply.

Sinbad took the lead, cutting through the brush with his scimitar. Tishimi kept pace right behind him, her hand never leaving the hilt of her sheathed sword. William and Henri followed, with Ralf taking up the rear of the party.

They hiked deep into the forest for what seemed like hours. Despite the relative lack of sunlight, the heat was as intense as the desert. The path was winding and they had no way of knowing if they were being led closer to their goal, into some unspeakable danger, or both. But still they continued moving forward.

Eventually, the group came to a clearing at the edge of a cliff face. A waterfall rushed forth from the ridge, emptying into a large lake. The water was the purest any of them had ever laid sight on, and they wasted no time in drinking of the liquid, splashing it on their faces and bodies to relieve themselves of the intense heat. Ralf and Henri even immersed themselves in the water, reveling in its cool feeling against their skin.

Sinbad cupped his hands to drink of the water. The liquid appeared to defy the intense heat, feeling as cold as ice. And that simple fact concerned him slightly. What's more, he noticed the Grachene has returned to his sash, vibrating as harshly as it had before.

"That's enough!" he barked. "Be on alert!"

Tishimi and William snapped to attention immediately, while Henri and Ralf were a bit slower to respond. But still, they quickly emerged from the lake and drew their own weapons as well. Sinbad took the scimitar from its scabbard and with his free hand, gripped the Grachene.

There was a demonic wail and the five warriors prepared themselves. The sound came from above them and figures jumped off the ridge. They were silhouettes against the sky, until they hit the ground and their forms could be more clearly discerned.

All of them were burly, brutish beings, with horns protruding from the sides of their heads. They wore only loincloths of animal skins, with a large pointed tooth on each end of their lips. Their skin had a reddish tint, taut muscles tightening beneath its surface. In their hands, each held a club made of a metal that reflected the light off its surface.

"Tishimi, do you know what these things are?" asked William.

"Oni," she said.

They brandished their clubs, and their yellow eyes blazed with anger towards the trespassers on their territory. One stepped forward, pointing his club at the crew. "This is your one warning...leave this place and go back to whence you came."

Sinbad responded by hurling the Grachene and it struck the demon right between his eyes. He fell back, dead before he struck the ground. The other oni protested with growls and snarls of hatred.

"I think you've upset them, Captain," said Ralf.

"T'would appear so, Mr. Gunarson."

The oni attacked from all sides and the crew fought back bravely. The quarters were far too close for Henri to use his bow, so instead he relied on a sword slimmer than that utilized by Ralf or William and capable of being wielded single-handedly. He drove it into the neck of the oni who came close to him, drawing it out just as quickly as the beast fell, then deflecting the strike from a second oni's club. Henri parried each strike from the oni's club with a smile on his face, toying with the demon before he somersaulted over the oni's head and drove his sword into his back.

In reveling in his own glory, Henri failed to notice a third oni creep up on him from behind. But fortunately, Ralf had, and the Norseman wrapped his arm around the oni's neck, pulling it to him while driving his broadsword into his back. Ralf pulled the sword out and smiled at Henri.

"Careful, Frenchman. I may not be there next time."

Tishimi exchanged strikes with an oni, deflecting his attacks with her sword. The oni had managed to push her up against the face of the cliff, and she had no escape. The oni charged at her and Tishimi spun to the side. She completed her twirl and came around to the front. The oni turned as well and once he had, he was rewarded with Tishimi's sword driven into his heart, pushing him up against the cliff.

William found himself facing off against two of the oni, trying as best he could to parry the strikes from both with just his one sword. Although he had managed to give as good as he got, he was quickly growing weary and knew that he could not keep up this assault much longer. It was Sinbad who came to his rescue, the sailor tackling one of the oni into the lake and holding his head under until he ceased moving.

With that distraction, William was able to regain his footing against the remaining opponent, his broadsword striking down each attempted attack from the oni's club. Now, it was the Scotsman who had obtained the upper hand and the oni who was quickly losing ground. William twirled his sword around the oni's club, moving faster until the oni's grip faltered and he was left without a weapon. It was then that the Scotsman spun forward, swinging his sword around and severing the oni's head.

Sinbad stood in the pond, moving away from the corpse. He approached the oni he'd killed with the Grachene and bent down, taking the dagger by its hilt and pulling it from his victim's skull. Tishimi washed the blood from her sword in the waterfall before sheathing it in the scabbard.

"This reminds me of the legend of Onigashima, where those creatures roam free," she said.

"I thought this was Yamatai?" asked William.

"It could be either, or it could be both." Tishimi pushed her hands up against the cliff from which the water fell. She felt for grips and when she found them, began to scale. "Only one way to be certain."

The men looked to Sinbad and he nodded his agreement, being the first to follow Tishimi up the cliff. The others moved after him, scaling the surface until they reached the summit. What they found was that the waterfall was the end of a river that led further inland. Tishimi was the first to begin walking along the bank, and the rest chased after her.

The river led them up to a plateau, where it ended in a small moat, encircling a stone dais. Atop that platform was a series of ruins; stone tablets with strange markings upon their faces. Three statues, carved in the shape of guardians and with the points of their massive swords resting at their feet, surrounded the small moat. Tishimi studied each of the monuments several times, looking over the characters and thinking hard on their true meaning. The language was difficult, and though it was similar to what she had been trained in, it was also very different.

"Can you understand this?" asked Henri.

"The language is…paradoxical," said Tishimi. "But the pictographs tell a far more coherent story."

"What can you tell of them?" asked Sinbad.

"The pictographs are clearly of Himiko," said Tishimi.

"Does it say anything of the treasure?" asked Henri.

William cast him a glare of annoyance and the Frenchman shrugged. "What? I cannot be the only one thinking it."

"Henri poses a point," said Sinbad. "We came here seeking Himiko's treasure. If it is not present, has this all been for naught?"

"The treasure is here, it is only a matter of finding it." Tishimi moved between the various structures, reading and re-reading the characters inscribed on them.

"You're making me dizzy," said Ralf.

"There's more," said Tishimi, ignoring her teammate's comment. "They hint that Himiko's death was not natural. Instead, it was the gods who feared her power and they were responsible for the isolation of Yamatai in the Ma no Umi. As her subjects died off one by one, Himiko was left with naught but her valued riches and the cursed souls as her guardians. Her kingdom became her prison."

"So the jikininki, the oni, the storm…?" asked William.

"They were intended to keep us out, but also to keep Himiko in," said Tishimi. "They were her guardians and we have breached the prison walls."

"So if this is her prison, where then is her cell?" asked Sinbad.

"Give me time, this text is difficult to read."

Ralf folded his burly arms and glanced down at his feet. When he did, he noticed something strange about the dais. For one, it was as if there were a series of pieces as opposed to one, with concentric circles leading towards the center. Two, the different pieces had lines carved into them, but the lines did not connect. Ralf followed the lines, moving closer to the center where there were no carvings. Henri watched the large man move about and groaned.

"What game are you playing at now?" he asked. "I know you are impatient for battle, but try to keep still."

"Not that, look down."

Henri squinted in confusion but then did as Ralf said. He too saw the same disconnected lines that his friend had. Sinbad and William followed their example, and Tishimi glanced briefly, but still concentrated on the tablets. She began to notice a connection between the tablets and the lines.

"…this text is difficult to read."

"The story is disjointed. We must arrange it in the correct order." Tishimi went to one of the tablets and looked up.

"Arrange? How do you expect us do to that?" asked Henri.

Tishimi gripped the tablet in both hands and pushed against it. As she expected, it was not anchored to the ground. "The tablets can be removed. And on this is where the story begins."

"Where does it go?" asked William. "There appears to be no start point."

"Earlier, you called Himiko the Sun Queen?" asked Sinbad.

Tishimi gave a nod, which was quickly followed by a growing, knowing smile. "Of course! It must point to the east. The rise of the sun, like the rise of the Sun Queen. Ralf?"

Ralf moved to the tablet and wrapped two meaty hands around its stone surface. He pulled and the tablet gave. Tishimi led him to the point closest to the east. William met her there and raised that tablet from its mounting, laying it gently on the ground. Ralf inserted the one he held into the now-vacant slot.

"Did it work?" asked Henri.

"Maybe we won't know until we've finished," said Tishimi.

"Or maybe this is just a massive waste of time."

Tishimi ignored the Frenchman. "Come, let us find the next one."

She directed the crew to the next successive part of the story, inserting that tablet to the left of the first. They continued on until all the tablets had been rearranged into their correct order, an ordeal that took an hour or more to complete. Once they had finished, Ralf knelt by the moat, splashing the cool water on his face.

Henri gave a huff. "All that work and nothing has changed."

"What work?" asked William. "All you did was stand there and complain the whole time."

Henri waved off the criticism with his hand. "All I'm saying is we seem to be right where we started and..."

The ground began to rumble as the parts of the dais moved beneath their feet. The group was nearly thrown to the ground, but they reacted quickly and jumped off the dais. Now unencumbered the dais moved of its own will until the carved lines on its surface moved into their proper space. The innermost circle slid down, and light emanated from the opening it created. As they looked upon the dais, they knew what the lines meant; they formed a pictograph of the sun.

Once they dropped down into the opening made by the center column, they found stone steps arranged in a spiral. No torches were present, and yet the staircase was perfectly lit by some supernatural means. Sinbad took the lead, drawing his scimitar as he moved down the steps. He risked a look to his sash and experienced some small relief when he saw the Grachene was not present.

The stairs went on for a great distance and they were now deep into the plateau. Still they went on further, and all the crew were uneasy. After a long hike, they were finally rewarded by reaching the foot of the steps. Ahead of them was an archway that connected to a wide tunnel. The keystone was adorned with a carving of a woman, her head framed by the rising sun.

"It appears we are on the right path," said Sinbad.

They said nothing, just continued walking. The strange light still bathed the tunnel, guiding their path. When the tunnel ended, it was in a large chamber. Ancient statues and weapons encrusted with precious gemstones lined the walls, open chests contained an uncountable number of gold coins, and there were numerous other items, jewelry, tools, small figures, all made of rare materials. Henri let out a laugh upon the site of the treasure and immediately went to one of the chests, examining the coins within. All of them were adorned with the figure of the sun on both sides. Ralf joined in his friend's revelry, moving for the ancient weapons along the walls and testing them out. William wandered about the chamber, examining the artifacts but in a far more restrained manner.

"The treasure of Himiko," said Tishimi, staring in wonder.

Sinbad saw the look in her eyes and smiled as he patted her on the shoulder. "And it is all because of you."

Henri came up to them, struggling to contain several items in his arms. "Sinbad, we should send for the rest of the crew, yes? We cannot clear out this chamber by our lonesome!"

Sinbad looked out among the treasure and nodded. "I suppose so. Take what you can, we will return for the rest."

While the men gathered as much as they could carry, Tishimi walked through the chamber, moving over to the far wall where there existed a mural of Himiko. In the painting, her face was pale, dressed in an orange and red kimono. Her expression was stern and she held a staff, a jewel-encrusted crown adorning her head. In the center of the crown was a large white orb surrounded by flames, as if it were the sun itself.

Tishimi felt herself entranced by the orb in Himiko's crown, her eyes fixating on the flames. She could almost see them moving about, coming to life. The colors shifted, the brightness dazzling and blinding.

"Tishimi!"

She could hear the voice calling her name…was it Sinbad? It sounded so far in the distance. The call came again: "Tishimi!" It seemed further, like the whistling of wind in the distance. Tishimi…such an odd name. Who was Tishimi? It sounded like something from a half-remembered dream.

Sinbad tired of calling and moved towards her. "Tishimi, is something amiss?" An invisible force rammed against the captain, throwing him with such power that he landed outside the chamber, flat on his back. Ralf, William, and Henri immediately dropped the items they carried and rushed for Tishimi as well, but were ejected in the same manner as their captain.

"What manner of sorcery is this?" asked William.

There came a rumble and a wall lowered over the chamber's entrance. Sinbad quickly got to his feet and went for it, hoping to squeeze through. He called out as well "Tishimi!" but it was futile. Tishimi could not hear him and the wall prevented any entrance.

When Tishimi opened her eyes, she was staring up at the sun over the mountaintops. She heard them crying her name and she cast her eyes downward, looking out over the crowd. Hundreds of people bowed submissively before her, resting on their knees, their hands spread out on the ground and their heads nearly touching the dirt.

Her eyes fell to her garments. She was adorned in kimono of the finest silk, with jewels hanging from her neck. Her right arm was extended to the side and gripped in that hand was a staff carved from jade. She could also feel the weight of a crown upon her head.

Men surrounded her, her royal guard, adorned with armor and holding spears. And though the people bowed to her, she could feel the fear emanating from them. It was not the guards whom they feared, though, but her own power. They continued to chant her name.

"Himiko! Himiko! Himiko!"

Himiko, yes. That was her name. And this was Yamatai, her kingdom. Soon, she would expand its borders; bring order to the surrounding nations. Yamatai would be a model for the rest of the world to follow, a prime example of peace through order and discipline.

But there was a strange weight at her side. She looked down and saw a sword sheathed by her side, resting in the obi. Why would she have need for a sword? Even if not for her retainers, her magicks were powerful enough to destroy anyone who would be foolish enough to attack her. But there was something about the blade that called to her, and she could hear a whistling of wind, as if the sword was trying to speak to her.

Ti…shi…mi…

This strange voice captured her attention and she could concentrate on nothing else. She reached for the sword and when she gripped the hilt, everything changed. She was now somewhere different, in a new place.

No…it was where she was before.

Tishimi was back in the chamber, surrounded by the treasure. She saw the wall covering the exit and ran to it, pushing up her hands against the stone surface. The warrior woman felt along the expanse, trying to find a switch or release to open the door.

"Sinbad!" she called out but heard no response.

"What makes you think they will wait for you?"

The voice was soft, almost lyrical. Tishimi spun and reached for her sword. She fixed her gaze on the mural, and distortions appeared in the air around it. The painting became more three-dimensional and moved closer towards her. The mural transformed into a woman, who stepped free from the wall that was her prison.

"Himiko," said Tishimi.

The Sun Queen gave a smile at the recognition and offered a slight bow.

"Where are my friends?"

"Friends?" asked Himiko. "Is that what you call them?"

"What have you done with them? Answer me, witch!"

"Why do you think I would have done anything to them? Perhaps they simply left you here?"

Tishimi shook her head. "No, they wouldn't."

Himiko approached closer. When she moved, though, there was no movement of the kimono at her feet. Like she floated. "These so-called friends, the ones you avoid? The ones you stand apart from?"

Tishimi relaxed her stance, her hand falling away from her sword.

"You are an outsider on that ship, sister. Not because you wish it, but because they fear you. It was why they objected to you joining the crew in the first place. It is why they are constantly leery of you. Because they fear the power you possess."

"Power?" At first, Tishimi's eyes carried nothing but anger and distrust for the Sun Queen. But now, it had morphed into a kind of curiosity.

"Indeed, power." Himiko's eyes were like shining emeralds, matching those of Tishimi's. Any who viewed the two of them together might mistake them for twins. "You have power, sister. Power that men fear. Because it is power that can reduce them to dust."

Himiko held her arms out, her fingers stretching out towards Tishimi. "Join me. Together, we may combine our power. Destroy all those who would see us crushed beneath their heels. Surely there are those you wish to see punished."

Tishimi considered that. There was a man, long ago. "Kamito."

Himiko nodded. "How long have you sailed with Sinbad? How long have you helped those men on their quests? Has there been any mention of aiding you on yours? Come, take my hands. There will be no cave he can hide in when we combine our power."

The temptation was great. Tishimi moved closer, raising her hands towards Himiko. Each of them approached the center, their fingers almost touching. Tishimi's skin brushed up against Himiko's and she could feel incredible warmth there. And Himiko's smile widened.

"Yes, my sister. Join with me. Become one with me."

Then the voice, again.

Tishimi...mana-musume...

It was a voice she hadn't heard in years, a voice that seemed to come from her sword. And when she heard it, Tishimi's mind was taken back to that final time she heard the mysterious voice.

She was still a girl, barely a teenager. And when she returned from her tutors one day, there were bodies scattered around her father's workshop. Tishimi ignored them, however, and searched for the only man she cared of...Tokami Osara, her father.

He barely clung to life, blood freely escaping from his wounds with every breath. His fingers were wrapped tightly around the blade of the sword he had been crafting. Tokami held the sword up with the hilt pointed at his daughter. Her questioning eyes fell to his and he gave her a simple nod.

Tishimi took the hilt, but as she pulled it away, Tokami gripped the blade tight enough that it cut into his hand. She stopped, but he just smiled at her. "This must be done."

Tishimi shook her head, trying to hold back the tears she felt welling in her eyes. "No, we must get you to a doctor."

"Mana-musume, I haven't much time, so listen closely," he said. "My blood...you must wash the blade in it."

"No, that's madness..."

"Through that simple act, I shall always remain with you. I shall always protect you." He took her free hand and clamped it against one of the many wounds on his body. Tishimi wept, feeling the sticky warmth of her father's blood. Once he released her hand, she raised it from his body, and held it up, the crimson fluid dripping from her fingers. She hesitated, but Tokami urged her on.

"Do it."

Tishimi was still reluctant, but she wrapped her fingers around the blade and moved down it, smothering the sword in the blood of its craftsman. When she finished, she looked back down at Tokami, and he weakly smiled at her.

"Always remember...you wield Osara steel not only in your hand, but also in your heart."

Tishimi opened her eyes, staring at Himiko. She pulled away from the Sun Queen, moving back into a battle stance and reaching for her sword.

"No, what are you doing?" asked Himiko, concern falling over her face. "Are you mad?"

Tishimi drew the same sword that years earlier she washed in the blood of her father. She took hold of the hilt with both hands and held it at the ready, fixing an angry glare on her opponent. "You think I am some child, easily led astray. You think you can play on my desire for vengeance while ignoring the values instilled in me?"

"Values of a dying world. One that would see us oppressed."

Tishimi shook her head. "My father trained me as fiercely as he would any male warrior. He gave no quarter, nor did I ask for any. This sword is infused with his onryo, because he knew only I was worthy enough to bring suffering to the man who killed him. My hatred for Kamito cannot be separated from my father's grudge, and my father's grudge cannot be separated from the daughter he raised. A daughter who would never bow before anyone, not even a goddess."

Himiko dropped her arms and her concerned face morphed into one wracked with anger. Her emerald eyes became like the burning center of the sun and she raised her hands to her sides. "I shall not be denied my escape!"

Tishimi charged forward, raising her sword. She ran it through Himiko, pushing until the tip struck the wall where the Sun Queen's mural was once contained. The warrior pulled the sword free and Himiko's body collapsed at her feet. "Yes, you shall."

A rumbling came from behind and Tishimi turned to see the chamber entrance opening. On the other side were her teammates, still waiting for her. They came towards her, relief plainly evident on their faces.

"Tishimi!" said Sinbad, his exuberance barely concealed. "We worried you might be lost to us."

"No," she said, but looked back at the spot where Himiko's body was. She could tell, even from that distance, that only her clothing remained. The woman who was clad in the garments was gone. "But I fear we may all be if we do not move, and fast."

"What do you mean?" asked William.

"Defeating Himiko was far too easy, it can only mean she has something far worse in mind for us," said Tishimi. "We must return to the Blue Nymph immediately!"

"Why are we leaving? We rescued Tishimi, and there is a treasure waiting to be pillaged!" said Henri. During the trek back up the steps and even now as they emerged out onto the stone dais at the top of the plateau, he had never ceased his complaints for a single second.

"What do you mean we rescued Tishimi?" asked Ralf. "It was her own actions that resulted in her freedom!"

"The specifics are unimportant, all that matters is we came for a treasure and now we are leaving before we've claimed it!"

"We have no other option," said Tishimi. "Himiko will not allow us to leave this island alive."

"But you killed her!" said Henri.

"Chigau, all I did was break her hold over me. If it were that simple to kill Himiko, her power would not still control this island."

"I hate to agree with the Frenchman, but this seems much like a coward's play," said Ralf.

Tishimi's eyes blazed with anger. "It is not cowardice. Himiko's power is greater than you realize."

"No Gunarson has ever fled from a battle, regardless of the danger. If I am to die battling this witch, then I shall enter Valhalla a warrior."

While the three argued, Sinbad crossed his arms and stared at the stone sentries lining the moat around the dais. He rubbed his beard in thought, looking at each of the granite warriors. William, desiring to separate himself from the bickering, made an inquiry.

"What is it?"

With the hand that had stroked his facial hair, Sinbad pointed at one of the statues. "Do you remember what pose these sentries held when we arrived?"

William furrowed his brow as he tried to remember. "Are they different?"

Sinbad nodded. "Before, the swords were pointed at the ground. But now…"

"Now the blades aim skyward."

"Precisely. Am I simply misremembering?" asked Sinbad.

The stone soldier's eyes came to life, burning with a bright crimson glow. It raised its sword higher and brought it down towards the captain. Sinbad crossed his arms over his head, bracing them against the soldier's hands. The muscles in Sinbad's arms tightened as he tried to keep the soldier from pushing down further, but his strength would not last much longer.

William swung his broadsword at the sentry's back and it diverted its attention from Sinbad to the Scotsman. The soldier thrust forward with his blade and William had to jump to the side to avoid the strike.

The commotion drew the attention of the other three. Tishimi rushed to William's aid, while a second sentry came to life and attacked Ralf. Henri readied his bow. The archer reached behind his back for his quiver, and a stone hand wrapped around his wrist, hefting him into the air. Henri struggled in its grip, feeling the bones in his wrist on the verge of being ground into dust. He swung in the sentry's grip, pushing his feet off against its head and swinging back again, each time building up more momentum. On his final swing, there was enough of a kick-back that the soldier's head rocked and his grip loosened.

Henri fell to the ground, and Sinbad came to his aid with the power of his scimitar. The sharp blade sent bits of rock flying off the guardian, but it returned Sinbad's strikes with its own. Sinbad connected his weapon with the sentry's, the two of them locked in a stalemate. Henri stepped back from the battle, trying to get enough distance to fire his arrows. As he backed away, he quickly ran out of ground and nearly lost his footing at the edge of the plateau. Henri jumped back onto solid ground before he could slip, and then had an idea. He notched an arrow and fired it at the guardian.

The stone soldier pushed Sinbad away and faced the archer. It charged towards Henri and the Frenchman stood his ground, smiling. The sentry came closer, holding out its weapon, but Henri leaped at the last moment, bounding off its head. The soldier didn't have the same dexterity as Henri and could not stop itself before it tumbled from the top of the plateau.

Tishimi and William exchanged blows with the second soldier. William's movements were slower, although his strikes more powerful. Tishimi's power was in her speed rather than her strength, and she could deliver quick, strategic blows as William continued to provide the distraction. But Tishimi knew it would take more than their steel to defeat this brute. William had realized it as well, and then he spotted something else.

He deflected a strike from the soldier and gestured to the center of the dais, where the entrance to the cavern was. "Tishimi!"

She saw it and nodded, understanding her teammate's plan. Tishimi slashed the soldier's back, and it turned from William. Tishimi ran for the center of the dais and waited before the entrance. The sentry came at her and she deflected its slashes. Tishimi rolled on the ground and the sentry stumbled, falling into the entrance. As it began to pull itself out, there was a rumbling. The ground moved and the entrance started to close, right upon the guardian. William dropped the tablet he had removed from the slot, letting it fall to the ground.

Ralf's axe-swings were swifter than one would think, given the man's size. But still not quick enough to strike his target. He continued relentlessly, and the soldier was having trouble evading. The sentry raised its weapon to deflect, but when Ralf's axe struck, the sword was reduced to pebbles. The warrior looked down at the remnants of its weapon and tossed it aside, raising its fists. Ralf snickered and dropped his axe as well. He then drew his broadsword, only to discard it. The Norseman cracked his knuckles.

"Come on, then!"

The soldier rushed him and Ralf braced himself for the strike. The soldier tackled him to the ground and the two behemoths rolled in the grass before splashing in the river. It was the sentry who landed on top and pummeled Ralf's head, bruises and cuts quickly forming along the giant's skin. But even in the face of that assault, and with his face bloodied and tender, he still managed to laugh. The sentry seemed a bit taken aback by this, and then Ralf grabbed its neck and flipped over. Now it was Ralf's turn, and he returned every blow the sentry gave him. His knuckles may

The soldier...tumbled from the top of the plateau...

have been flesh and bone, yet they struck with such force they may as well have been granite, just like his foe's.

Ralf stood and pulled up the sentry. Mustering all his strength, he threw the sentry towards the dais, and it struck one of the tablets, knocking it free. Ralf approached as the soldier began to rise and he retrieved the tablet. Raising it above his head, he drove it into the sentry's back, repeating the action until the soldier was broken in two.

The crew regrouped and Tishimi glared at Ralf. "Has your thirst for battle been sated yet?"

"Perhaps not entirely, but it'll do," said Ralf.

Tishimi spun to Henri. "And are you ready to concede I was correct about the dangers this island still poses?"

Henri scoffed, then under his breath, muttered, "I suppose these baubles will suffice."

"Very well, then we shall return to the Blue Nymph," said Sinbad. "Gather your belongings, we leave immediately."

They encountered no resistance as they retreated from the plateau, returning back to the lake where they encountered the oni, their bodies still lying dead where they'd been left. The crew proceeded on; moving back through the jungle, following the path Sinbad had cleared earlier with his scimitar.

During their journey, Tishimi paused briefly and cast her eyes skyward. The sky had now darkened, with red clouds forming. Thunder rang out, like an angry yell. Himiko was not finished yet, Tishimi knew that much. So far, their progress had been relatively easy when considering Himiko's great power. She would not give up so easily, not after the crew of the Blue Nymph had absconded with her treasure and ruined her chance at escape.

A hand on her shoulder nearly caused Tishimi to draw her blade, but she relented when she realized it was Sinbad. His eyes turned to the clouds as well and then back to the lady. "Come, we must depart."

"It isn't over yet," said Tishimi.

"So it would seem." Sinbad moved ahead and Tishimi followed. They reconnected with the rest of the crew and made it to the edge of the jungle. Just ahead was the white sand of the beach. The quintet ran from the green and out into the open. In short order, they reached the bank where the water washed on the shore. In the distance, they could see the azure sails of their home. But something else was wrong.

"Where's the boat?" asked Ralf, referring to the small boat they'd taken from the Blue Nymph to shore.

"Are we at the correct spot?" asked Henri. "Did we take a different path from the jungle?"

Sinbad waded into the water and found something floating. He bent down and retrieved it, raising the soaked, broken piece of wood to his eyes. Just as quickly, he tossed it back into the water. "The boat was here, and it was destroyed."

"Those damn ogres!" spat Henri.

"Come, we must swim," said Sinbad. "The Blue Nymph is not far."

"But the treasure...?"

"Hang the damn treasure, Delacrois!" shouted William.

Further into the water they waded, as far as they could manage before it deepened. Sinbad dove in first, swimming beneath the water and pushing ahead. The others followed, except for Henri, who paused. He stuffed his quiver with as much of the treasure as it could carry and paddled after his mates, keeping his head above water.

Sinbad's strokes were broad and quick, propelling him ahead of the others. With the darkened skies, the water appeared almost black. Sinbad surfaced, unable to see beneath the water any longer. But his senses of perception were so great that he could detect the slight shift of the current. Sinbad stopped and turned, treading water to keep his head above the waves. But try as he might, he could see no sign of anything amiss.

He felt the current shift again and he spun, and still found nothing. The others swam closer, their eyes alight with questions. The uncertainty on their captain's face was not a look they were used to, and though none would give an admission, it frightened them.

"There is something here," he said.

"Sinbad!" cried Ralf.

Sinbad felt the wave rising and spun again. Except it wasn't a wave, but rather a serpent of some sort, rising above the water. Yellowish-green scales lined its body and its massive jaw opened, revealing rows of sharpened ivory and a forked tongue snaked out, tendril-like appendages hanging from its snout like a mustache. The dragon rose above Sinbad and dove with its open mouth crushing down around the warrior, the two disappearing beneath the water.

"No!" Tishimi dove after them.

"Tishimi!" cried William, but it was too late to stop her.

A moment later, Tishimi burst through the surface. "Useless, I cannot see a thing."

"What was that?" asked Henri.

"It seemed to resemble Jörmungandr," said Ralf.

"Dragon," said Tishimi. "They are rumored to exist in these waters."

"And when were you planning to tell us that?" asked Henri.

"I said there were dangers, I could not confirm whether or not they were true," said Tishimi.

"We cannot let that serpent take Sinbad without exacting vengeance!" shouted Ralf. "We must..."

The current picked up and they faced the rising tide rapidly approaching them. The dragon's dorsal fins broke through the surface, its back arching and ascending. The head came last, its eyes with the same glow as the other creatures they faced. But the dragon appeared to struggle keeping its jaw closed. The beast's head thrashed above the waves and finally, the jaw opened. And Sinbad stood in the center of those teeth, his arms held above him and bent at the elbows, trying with all his might to pry open the mouth.

Henri swam to the serpent's side and took an arrow from the quiver, stabbing it into its side. The dragon wailed in pain and Sinbad jumped from its maw, catching one of the tendrils. He used it as a rope, swinging up and then releasing it, flipping and grabbing hold of the dragon's brow. Sinbad perched himself on its head, crouching low to maintain his balance. He took his scimitar and jammed it into the dragon's eye. Its screams were like the sound of a thousand wailing souls and it flailed its head. Sinbad wasted no more time, springing from the beast's snout and diving back into the water.

The dragon rose higher from the waves, its arms breaching the surface. It pulled the scimitar free, but the damage was done and black blood dripped from the socket where its eye once was. The dragon grit its teeth and a deep growl could be heard from within its body. Worse, smoke billowed from its nostrils.

"DIVE!" cried Tishimi.

When the dragon's mouth opened again, it spat out a stream of flames, flames that were avoided by the crew following their lady's orders and seeking refuge beneath the water. The dragon dove after them, disappearing completely in the inky blackness of the Devil's Sea.

The crew came up for air, but now the waters were still once more.

There was no sign of the dragon. And other than the heat of the water, it seemed to any who looked upon the scene that there never was a dragon.

"Where did it go?" asked Henri. "Is it dead?"

"Unlikely, I only injured it," said Sinbad. "But maybe that was enough to frighten it off."

"Ho, Sinbad!"

Sinbad smiled and saw his ship approaching. Haroun waved at them from the mast and the crew stood on the deck, cheering. Rafi stood there with them, and tossed a rope out to the water. Sinbad caught it and hoisted himself up, planting his feet on the teakwood surface and climbing until he pulled himself over the rail. The rest of his team followed, and they were all granted a hero's welcome once they came aboard.

When asked what they'd found, Henri emptied his quiver of the treasure he was able to hold on to. "Not as much as I'd hoped, but a decent enough haul, I suppose."

Sinbad laughed and slapped the Frenchman on the back. "It will never be enough for you, my friend."

"Tell us the tales of the adventure!" said one of the younger men on the crew as he and several others gathered around Ralf.

"Of course, my friends!" said Ralf. "But first, is there any of that sake left?"

Rafi approached William, who was wringing water out of his clothing as best he could. "Seems quite the ordeal you went through."

"Fortunately, we had no need for your medicines," said William.

"No fortune, though." Rafi gave a knowing smile. "You must be disappointed."

William gave a chuckle. "Very funny, old man."

Sinbad proceeded to the quarterdeck, where Omar held the wheel. As he approached his first mate, the elder man just sneered at him. "I hoped to be rid of you for good this time. Make a respectable career for myself. Pursue safe trading, no more wild adventures."

Sinbad laughed. "It seems Allah is not one for granting your wishes, old friend."

"He has indeed laid a curse upon us." Omar cracked a brief smile and released the wheel. The two friends embraced. Omar motioned to the wheel. "She's yours again, Captain."

Sinbad took hold of the wooden spokes but saw Tishimi leaning over the rail and still staring out to sea. He released the wheel and stepped away. "I'll leave her in your care for a little longer, old friend."

The captain descended the steps from the quarterdeck, sidling up beside Tishimi and leaning over, resting his arms on the railing, staring out into the approaching dusk. Tishimi did not acknowledge his presence with a word or even a glance, and the pair stared out in silence. After several moments of this, Sinbad was the first to speak.

"You seem disturbed."

"I do not believe it is over," said Tishimi.

"You said that before."

"And then we were attacked by living statues and a dragon."

Sinbad couldn't help the chuckle that escaped his lips. "Well met."

She looked at him, the joke apparently lost on her. "You make light of our predicament."

Sinbad frowned. "No, I'm simply enjoying the moment. I understand your concerns and whether you believe it or not, I do indeed share them. However, we cannot let our fear of another calamity prevent us from living. If Himiko wishes to attack us, she shall. I can worry or I can relax, neither action will sway her one way or another."

The boat hit a rough patch and Sinbad and Tishimi had to grip the rail to avoid stumbling. Sinbad turned his gaze to the quarterdeck. "Omar, I would not have given you the helm if I thought you would sail with the skill of a drunken child!"

"Wasn't me, Sinbad! I saw no indication of any ill waters!"

"You were saying?" asked Tishimi.

Sinbad called out to the crew. "Gather 'round! We still have some obstacles ahead. If we're to escape the Devil's Sea, we must be prepared for any eventuality." He reached behind his back, remembering that his scimitar was lost in his fight with the dragon. Sinbad took the scimitar and drew it from a crewman's scabbard. "And I have need of your weapon."

"What do you need of us, Sinbad?" asked William.

"Stay alert, all of you," was the order. "Henri, climb the mast. Haroun as well. The two of you have the sharpest eyes on the ship, time to put them to use."

"Aye, Captain." Haroun took a lantern and nearly jumped for the ropes on the port side, climbing around them and ascending them with a natural skill. Henri went to follow him, but Sinbad gave him a final command.

"Henri, your arrows may need something extra."

"*Qui*," said Henri, taking the bow and sliding it onto his back beside his quiver. He also took one of the sake bottles before climbing the ropes on the starboard side, moving quickly to catch up to Haroun's speed.

Sinbad gripped the scimitar and went to the ship's fore. He placed one sandaled foot on the rail and leaned against his knee, watching out to the sea ahead of them. Tishimi was by his side, the sword designed by her father held in her hand.

"There's movement!" shouted Haroun from the mast. "Dead ahead!"

Sinbad squinted, but with the blackness of the water, he had trouble seeing as well as the younger man. The ship was hit by the side, and it drifted with the strike. Omar struggled with the wheel, trying to get back on course. Ralf ran to the other side, his weight helping to prevent the Blue Nymph from capsizing.

As the ship righted, the dragon rose from the water again. From the mast, Henri drew the string back on his bow, pulling the notched arrow with it. Haroun held the lantern's fire up to the alcohol-soaked cloth that surrounded the arrow and it burst into flame. Henri fired the flaming arrow and it soared like a beacon through the darkness, hitting the dragon between its eyes. It flayed in the ocean, shaking off the attack.

"Again!" ordered Sinbad.

Henri obliged, Haroun lighting another arrow and the archer letting it fly through the night. This one struck the dragon against the side of its head. The dragon's remaining eye burned with anger and it clasped its jaw tight, smoke billowing like plumes from the nostrils.

"Omar, turn!" shouted Sinbad.

Omar spun the wheel with all his might, but as the dragon rose further in the air, the water beneath the Blue Nymph rushed in to fill the open space, pulling the ship with it. Sinbad knew he had to do something to protect his ship and his crew. And so he ran for one of the ropes, cutting it free from the rail. He climbed onto the rope nets and jumped, swinging from the rope around the Blue Nymph. Sinbad released the rope and somersaulted in the air, moving in front of the dragon's eyesight.

The beast evidently recognized the man who had taken its eye, as it seemed to ignore the ship. Instead, it unleashed its flaming jet at Sinbad's free-falling figure. The flames missed him, but before Sinbad could strike the water, the dragon's clawed hand caught him and raised him up.

Its grip may as well have been iron shackles. Though Sinbad strained against it, the dragon had the captain at his mercy. It lifted him up so they could lock eyes. Smoke billowed from the nostrils, but this seemed to be more of anger than intent. The dragon tightened its claw, and Sinbad felt his bones giving, his blood flow being restricted.

Then, the dragon inexplicably unleashed a howl of agony and released

Sinbad. He fell into the ocean, striking the water somewhat motionless, struggling to move in light of the recent ordeal. A strong hand took hold of Sinbad's vest and pulled him towards the surface. William broke through the water, tugging Sinbad up with him and wrapping his arm around his captain's chest. He held to Sinbad, swimming back to the ship where Ralf raised Sinbad from the water with one hand.

Sinbad sat up, against the protests of Rafi, his concern being with the dragon. And upon close scrutiny, he could make out the lithe figure moving about the dragon's body. Tishimi had evidently jumped onto the creature, striking it with her sword in order that it would release Sinbad and focus its attention on her.

Tishimi gripped onto the dragon's mane as it flailed about, trying to shake her free. It was a difficult thing to manage, but her grace and balance allowed her to swing back onto solid footing and make another strike against the dragon's head. The dragon used its tail to propel itself as high as possible, and then the two of them crashed back beneath the sea.

Tishimi was beneath the water, and despite the darkness, she could see the dragon perfectly as it dove after her. She swam lower, kicking as fiercely as possible, pushing off with additional thrust just as the dragon's jaws were in snapping distance.

And there beneath the waves, something changed. The dragon paused, its form changing. The landscape shifted as well, and they were standing atop a mountain overlooking the sea. They were in the courtyard of a mountain palace and surrounding them were oni, jikininki, and stone soldiers. The dragon had shrunk down to Tishimi's size, but the change was not yet finished.

The dragon's serpentine body moved like clay, reforming into something resembling a humanoid. It was a woman dressed in battle armor, her single eye glowing bright red and a crown with a bright fireball in its center adorning her head. Himiko raised her staff with both hands and pointed it at Tishimi.

"You are ruining everything!"

Tishimi gave no response, simply drew her blade. The time for words was now long over and Tishimi tired of Himiko's constant baiting. Now, the two would simply fight and be done with it. Tishimi rushed at her, swinging her sword around in a large arc. Himiko raised her staff to defend, then stepped to the side and pivoted, spinning the staff around to strike at Tishimi's back.

Tishimi was fast enough to match her counter, blocking the attack. She jumped back, and the second Tishimi's feet hit the ground, she thrust forward in a stabbing motion. Himiko jumped, seeming to float and her feet rested on Tishimi's blade for the shortest of instances before her leg snapped out and struck Tishimi's jaw.

The young warrior reeled from the blow. Himiko moved in with another blow, hitting Tishimi's right shoulder with such incredible strength that Tishimi couldn't help but screaming. Sweat formed on her face and her shoulder burned with pain. Her right arm now hung useless at her side and any attempts to move it were greeted with even greater pain. The most Tishimi could do was support the arm with her left hand, and she panted heavily.

"Poor, little outsider," said Himiko. "The physical pain you experience now simply matches the emotional pain you have felt for years. You know I can make it go away. All you need to do is give yourself to me. There is no other recourse…you either surrender, or you perish."

Tishimi felt a sensation running through her arm. It was as if energy coursed from her sword into her body. She tightened her grip on her arm and felt added strength from the sword. It gave her the opportunity to snap her arm back into place with a sickening sound that provoked no reaction from either Tishimi nor Himiko.

"I am the last of the Osara clan, a noble line of warriors," she said. "Many have tried to corrupt our lineage, but none have ever succeeded. And none ever shall."

Tishimi spun, twirling her sword, and it appeared to grow longer and larger. Her speed was so swift that she was like a blur on her approach to Himiko. It is said that the Sun Queen herself was blinded by Tishimi's movements and radiance, and she was paralyzed in her final moments before Tishimi's blade cut through Himiko's neck.

The sun broke through the dark clouds and the skies returned to normal. The waters appeared to lighten as well, changing from the previous inky blackness into a pure blue. The crew of the Blue Nymph cheered at their good fortune, but Sinbad was not yet satisfied.

A call from Haroun on the mast directed the crew's attention further ahead. Sinbad ordered the boat to move forward. They came upon a small islet where Tishimi rested on her laurels, enjoying the feel of the warm sun on her skin. But perhaps most amazing of all was the prize by her side. For right beside Tishimi was the head of the giant dragon that had attacked them, the sword powered by the grudge of her father embedded in its skull.

The End

Tishimi and the Legend of Yamatai

To be honest, I'm something of a fraud.

While most of the authors working in New Pulp were fans of the classic characters like Doc Savage, The Shadow, Conan the Barbarian, John Carter of Mars, etc., I was not. Oh, I'd heard the names of the characters, but being born in the early 80s and coming of age in the 90s meant that the pulp reprints many of my contemporary authors grew up reading were long out of print by the time I came along. I did, however, subsist on a steady diet of comic books and action movies (the latter somewhat influenced by my father and older brother).

In my teen years, I began writing fanfiction and during my tenure in that community, I became acquainted with a man who would later become a valued mentor and a trusted friend, and that man is Derrick Ferguson. Like myself, Derrick was a voracious consumer of comics and movies, but he also had a lifelong affinity for pulp fiction. It was through Derrick that I first discovered that pulp fiction was more than just an incredible film directed by Quentin Tarantino and was actually the kind of stuff I'd been reading, watchingand writing my entire life.

Through Derrick, I became acquainted with the New Pulp movement and that acquaintance later brought me into contact with Ron Fortier, the Captain of Airship 27. Ron was kind enough to provide me with one of the first reviews on my first New Pulp book, Love & Bullets, and since then, he's reviewed every one of my books for his Pulp Fiction Reviews website.

Ron mentioned at one point that he would like me to do something for Airship 27. I had nothing particular in mind—being a self-published author, I prefer to handle all aspects of publishing my original creations.

But given that Airship 27 publishes a large number of anthologies, I told him to keep me posted on any that he may think I'll be a good fit for.

In late 2013, I published SoulQuest, a sci-fi/fantasy adventure tale with steampunk trappings, inspired by video games like Final Fantasy VII. As usual, I sent Ron a copy of the book. Once he finished it, not only did he provide a very touching review, but also extended an invitation for me to write a story for Sinbad: The New Voyages series. Ron told me that while he read SoulQuest, he felt I would be a good fit, and he informed me that the stories were inspired by the Ray Harryhausen films—The 7th Voyage of Sinbad, The Golden Voyage of Sinbad, and Sinbad and the Eye of the Tiger. I also obtained a copy of the Arabian Nights, where Sinbad made his first appearance in literature.

I watched the first two Harryhausen films and found I vastly preferred John Phillip Law's portrayal of Sinbad to Kerwin Mathews, and Law's version is what I drew inspiration from. I told Ron I was interested and he provided me with the series bible.

The character who spoke the most to me was Tishimi Osara. Being a resident of Japan myself and a teacher of Japanese literature, and also an advocate of strong female heroes, I felt an affinity with Tishimi. Minority and female heroes are unfortunately very rare in not only pulp but action fiction in general, an oversight that I feel needs to be corrected. This, combined with my knowledge and affinity for Japan, led me to come up with a story focused on Tishimi.

Some historical notes will follow. These Sinbad stories are set during the time of Haroun al-Rashid, the Caliph of Baghdad, which places them in the late 700s/early 800s. In terms of Japanese history, this was at the dawn of the Heian-jidai (preceding the Kamakura-jidai and the rise of the samurai class). In Chinese and Japanese history, there's mention of an ancient country in Japan called Yamatai-koku or Yamaichi-koku, during the Yayoi-jidai (roughly four centuries prior to the period of this story). According to legend, Yamatai was ruled by a shaman queen named Himiko or Pimiko. The historicity of Himiko and the location of Yamatai continues to be very contentious in Japanese history.

For this story, I chose to combine the legend of Yamatai with the Dragon's Triangle. No doubt you know of the Bermuda Triangle, but what many don't know is that the Bermuda Triangle is just one of many so-called "vile vortices" that exist across the world (twelve to be exact). The Devil's Sea (Ma no Umi) or Dragon's Triangle (also called the Formosa Triangle) is considered to be one of these areas. Though I don't put much stock in the legitimacy of the vile vortices (most studies have concluded the claims of them being high danger zones to be extremely hyperbolic at best and outright fabrications at worst), they do make great settings for adventure tales on the high seas.

The earliest mentions of Yamatai and Himiko occur in ancient Chinese texts. The earliest mentions in Japanese texts mostly concern Yamatai and began in the late 600s/early 700s. For the purposes of this story, I used the logic that those in the imperial class would have more knowledge of Yamatai and Himiko, and that extended to Tishimi (though she wasn't part of that class, she was well-educated so it didn't feel like much of a stretch).

Obviously, many liberties have been taken. The Dragon's Triangle extends from Miyake Island and down into the Philippine Sea, whereas the proposed locations for Yamatai are often proposed as northern Kyushu, the Kinki region, or more recently, Nara. None of these regions are islands, nor located within the Dragon's Triangle, but for the purposes of this story, I decided to put Yamatai in the center of the Triangle. I'm also not the first to do this—the recent Tomb Raider video game also proposed the Dragon's Triangle as the location of Yamatai. The oryoshi in the story are mentioned as being imperial soldiers. Although many expect samurai, the samurai didn't come into being until around the middle of the Heian-jidai. Oryoshi were an organization of professional warriors, assigned to specific provinces. Again, liberties were taken with them (I don't know if they wore any sort of standard uniform or dress, but felt it was necessary so Tishimi could easily recognize them).

I took other elements from Japanese society and mixed them into this story. The jikininki are one such example, and though I portray them as closer to zombies than the wendigo-like creatures they are in Japanese folklore, I also attribute this to Himiko's control over them. The oni as well are featured, ogre-like creatures (in most depictions) from the island of Onigashima (Demon Island). Onigashima is featured in the classic Japanese folktale Momotaro, and I simply combined it with Yamatai. And of course, dragons are a classic staple of Japanese and Chinese folklore, often depicted as water spirits.

The most interesting thing for me was focusing on Tishimi and her place within the crew of the Blue Nymph. The bible for this series described Tishimi as being set apart from the rest of the crew, with some even resenting the fact that a woman is onboard. As I wrote the story, I felt a sense of kinship between Tishimi and William, given that they are the only two who aren't focused on glory or treasure. I wanted to explore who Tishimi was and get into her character a little more—why would this woman, who isn't interested in glory or treasure—stay on a ship where she is distant from the others? What might be the reason for that distance? I don't know that I've actually provided answers to these questions, but they were what drove my interest throughout writing the story.

Thanks for reading up to this point. If you enjoyed this story and the others contained in this collection, then please consider posting a review on the site you purchased from or on Goodreads. Reviews are a crucial component of indie publishing and we need as many of them as we can get. Thanks again.

PERCIVAL CONSTANTINE - Initially hailing from the northwest suburbs of Chicago, Percival Constantine is a graduate of Northeastern Illinois University and began his career first as an editor for Making Comics Studios. In 2007, he achieved his lifelong dream of writing and publishing a novel when he released his debut work, Fallen.

Since then, Percival has been active as a self-published author. He has two ongoing series of novellas. One is Infernum, focusing on an international organization of assassins. The other is The Myth Hunter, a globe-trotting adventure series that centers on Elisa Hill, a heroine who travels the world seeking out the truth behind the legends. In addition to those, he also writes two new series composed of short stories and novelettes—Luther Cross, dealing with a supernatural investigator for Pro Se Production's Pro Se Single Shot Signatures line and Vanguard, a superhero series that deals with a team of specials secretly gathered by the United States government to deal with the threats posed by a burgeoning superhuman community. Along with his fiction, Percival is also a contributing author for WhatCulture and a formatter for Pro Se Productions.

Visit PercivalConstantine.com for a complete list of Percival's work, and where you can also sign up for his mailing list to receive updates about discounts, freebies, beta-reading opportunities and other exclusives. As a bonus, all subscribers receive a free series starters books as a thank you for signing up. Currently, Percival resides in Japan's Kagoshima prefecture, working as a literature and writing instructor.

More seafaring adventure from
Airship 27 Productions: